DEBBIE MACOMBER

Promise Me Forever

She'd saved his life—
had she won his heart?

"I wouldn't want..."

"What wouldn't you want?" Sloan's voice was low and seductive as his hand cupped the other side of her face. "I can't help this," he whispered huskily. "Hate me later." His mouth gently kissed her chin, her eyes, the end of her nose, and caressed her cheek.

Joy should have stopped him. It wasn't him she'd hate later, but herself. Her arms slid around his neck; her fingers stroked the hair that grew thick there.

Sloan's mouth sought hers, and she moved her face against his until finally, when their lips met, Joy was beyond coherent thought.

Suddenly Joy emitted a small protesting sound, and Sloan tightened his hold and moved his mouth to the nape of her neck.

"Don't say it," he ground out in a fierce whisper. "I know what you're thinking."

"You couldn't possibly know."

"For once in your life, don't think. Feel."

Also available from MIRA Books and
DEBBIE MACOMBER

STARLIGHT
REFLECTIONS OF YESTERDAY

Coming soon

THE PLAYBOY AND THE WIDOW
FOR ALL MY TOMORROWS

DEBBIE MACOMBER

Promise Me Forever

MIRA BOOKS

ISBN 1-55166-052-0

PROMISE ME FOREVER

Copyright © 1985 by Debbie Macomber.

To Aunt Betty and Uncle Lavern,
Aunt Lois and Uncle Lynn.
This one's for you.

OREGON
IDAHO
CALIFORNIA
Redwood Empire
NEVADA
Sierra Nevada
San Francisco
Yosemite National Park
Death Valley
Fresno
Kings Canyon National Park
PACIFIC OCEAN
Sequoia National Park
ARIZONA
Oxnard
Sloan's House
Los Angeles
Chocolate Mts.
Salton Sea
San Diego
All underlined places are fictious.
MEXICO

One

Joy Neilsen brushed a dark strand of curly hair away from her face and straightened her shoulders. She stood in front of the closed door, strengthening her resolve. She'd been told what to expect. Absently her hand smoothed the crisp white pants of her nurse's uniform. This was a new case, and she couldn't help feeling apprehensive after listening to Dr. Phelps.

Determined, she forced a smile and opened the door. Quickly her brown eyes scanned the interior. Although the sun was shining, the drapes were closed and the room was filled with oppressive shadows. A solitary figure in a wheelchair stared silently into the distance.

With purpose-filled strides, Joy walked into the room.

"Good morning, Mr. Whittaker. I'm your

nurse, Miss Neilsen. I believe Dr. Phelps mentioned I was coming."

Silence.

Undeterred, Joy pulled open the drapes and paused momentarily to take in the beauty of the California coast. Huge waves crashed against the beach. The sky was the bluest of blue and not a cloud was in sight. Joy sighed her appreciation.

"Close the drapes." The harshly whispered words were barely discernible.

Joy decided to ignore him. No one had told her he was so young, mid thirties at most. His hair was dark and needed to be trimmed, his eyes were like that of a caged lion—fierce, and at the same time hopeless and angry. It wasn't difficult to see that this man had once been vital and proud. But he was close to being broken, and that was the reason she was here.

"It's a beautiful morning. I was up at dawn and saw the sunrise."

"I said close the drapes." There was no doubting the command a second time. The dark eyes squinted against the light.

"I'll be bringing your breakfast in a moment, if you'd like to get ready."

His mouth thinned, hardening his expression. Two large hands rotated the chair to her side.

"Would you like to eat on the deck?" she asked.

Ignoring her, he leaned forward, grabbed the drapes' pulley, and tugged them closed.

Expelling a frustrated sigh, Joy turned to him, hands on her hips. No, she wouldn't let this man get the better of her. It would be best for them both if he recognized early that she wasn't like the others.

The room was again dim, with only a minimum of soft light. Dragging a chair to the double glass doors, she unhooked the pulley, opened the drapes, and tossed the cord so that it caught on the valance.

"If you prefer to have the drapes closed, then do it yourself."

His eyes seemed to spit fire at her, but he said nothing. Although his face was covered with at least a day's growth of beard, Joy could see the nerve twitch in his lean jaw.

"I'll be back in five minutes with your breakfast," she informed him primly. She closed the door on her way out and paused to inhale a deep breath. Dr. Phelps hadn't un-

derstated the situation; Sloan Whittaker could
easily be her most difficult case.

The white-haired woman Joy had been introduced to earlier that morning glanced up
expectantly when Joy entered the large, modern kitchen.

"How'd it go?" Clara Barnes questioned
with speculative eyes.

"Fine," Joy answered with a weak smile.

As Clara chuckled, a network of wrinkles
broke out across her weathered brown face.
"I've been working for Mr. Whittaker too
many years to accept that. Odds are you won't
last the week." The cheery tone carried a heavy
note of challenge.

"I'll last." Joy laughed as she poured a glass
of juice and set it on the tray.

A brow flicked upward approvingly. "I said
to Mr. Whittaker's mother the minute I saw
you that you'd be the one to help Mr. Whittaker be his ol' self again."

"He has to help himself. There's only so
much you or me or anyone can do," Joy explained tightly, and lifted the breakfast tray.
She didn't mean to sound rude or discourag-
ing, but it was best to set the older woman
straight now. She wasn't a miracle worker.

"Mr. Whittaker's mother will be here this afternoon. I know she'll want to talk to you."

"Let me know when she arrives." The swinging kitchen door was opened with a push of her shoulder.

Sloan had wheeled across his room. He glanced up when she entered. His look was hard and unwelcoming; there was a grim line to his mouth. "I'm not hungry."

"No, I don't imagine you work up much of an appetite sitting in the chair, do you?"

Dark eyes flashed and narrowed menacingly.

"Well, if you're not hungry, I am." Joy walked onto the verandah and set the tray on the table. She made a small production of lifting the silver-domed food warmer. A thick slice of ham, two fried eggs, and hash-browns filled the plate. An order of toast was wrapped in a white linen cloth and set to the side. Joy deliberately slid the knife across the ham and lifted the first bite to her mouth. "Delicious," she murmured with closed eyes.

Twice she felt his gaze on her, but she said nothing. When she had finished, she stood and walked to the far side of the long deck. The view was fantastic. Sloan Whittaker must be more than bitter to block this beauty from his life. But then, she knew what it was to be immune to the lovelier things of life.

"I'll take the tray back to the kitchen and send Paul in to help you bathe."

He ignored the comment. "You didn't drink the orange juice." He reached up and lifted it from the tray. There was a suppressed violence about the way he handled the glass—as if he wanted to hurl it at her. "The hired help eat in the kitchen. Remember that."

She shouldn't have smiled. Joy realized that too late. Without warning he emptied the contents of the glass on her uniform. An involuntary gasp escaped as the cold liquid ran down her front. Calmly she set the tray aside. Their eyes clashed and held as she struggled to maintain control of her temper. "I'm sure that was an accident, Mr. Whittaker."

"And I assure you it wasn't." His hard gaze held hers with amused cynicism.

"That's unfortunate," Joy returned, and without a backward glance she emptied the remains of her lukewarm coffee in his lap. Not waiting for his reaction, she took the tray. "I'll send Paul in," she announced crisply, and left.

Her hands were trembling when she came into the kitchen. Sloan Whittaker's arrogant pride was definitely going to be a challenge. But he'd learn soon enough. The display of temper pleased her. He hadn't lost the will to fight. That was good; it was very good.

Clara looked up from the sink, the old eyes widening as she noted the juice stain.

Joy laid the tray on the counter and smiled wryly. "I had a small accident," she explained.

"Sure you did," Clara muttered with a dry laugh, and lifted the plate from the tray. "Well, I'll be. Mr. Whittaker ate his breakfast," she cried in open astonishment. "First time in six months that he's cleaned his plate. You are a miracle, girl. What did you do?"

Joy couldn't put a damper on the old woman's enthusiasm. "I'm afraid that's a professional secret, but I promise to let you in on it before I leave."

Smacking her lips, Clara beamed a brilliant smile. "I always said that once Mr. Whittaker started eating again he would walk. He won't ever be strong unless he eats."

"I couldn't agree with you more," Joy replied with a soft sigh. "But after such a large breakfast you should keep his lunch light. Nothing more than broth, but do me a favor and cook his favorite meal tonight.''

"I will, Miss, that I will.''

Pleased with herself, Joy walked down the hall to her room. She understood Sloan's frustration. His story was a familiar one. His car had skidded on a rain-slick road and smashed into a tree. The bare facts had been related by Dr. Phelps. Only when Joy pried further did she learn he had lain in the twisted wreck for hours in an agony beyond description before anyone found him. The initial surgery had saved his life, but in his weakened condition the operation to relieve the pressure on his spinal column had to be delayed. Months passed before he was strong enough to endure the next difficult surgery. Now there were no guarantees. Dr. Phelps told her there was feeling in Sloan Whittaker's legs, but the pain remained intense, and Sloan had decided to accept the wheelchair rather than endure the agony of learning to walk again.

Joy didn't need to be a psychologist to know that a man who resigned himself to a wheelchair had far more reason than pain. Something had happened to make him lose the will to use his legs. She'd know what it was before finishing this assignment.

After six months, the bitterness had built a thick wall around him. It wouldn't be easy to crack that granite fortress, but Joy was determined. She wanted to be the one to help him.

Entering her bedroom, she paused again to take in the expensive decor. The room was decorated in a powder-blue color scheme: the wallpaper contained tiny bluebells, the azure carpet was lush and full. The flowered bedspread matched the walls and drapes. Joy had seen pictures in magazines of rooms like this, but she'd never imagined she would be sleeping in one.

Money could buy a lot of things, and in Sloan's case it had bought him the privilege of choosing life in a deluxe model wheelchair.

Opening her closet, she took out and changed into a fresh uniform. She rinsed out the juice stain in the private bath off the bedroom. Once she'd turned off the water, she could hear the angry words coming from the room next to hers. Apparently Sloan wasn't in any better mood.

Paul had seemed the perfect type to deal with Sloan. He was an easygoing, laid-back sort of person who recognized a good thing when he saw one. His job entailed helping Sloan bathe and dress each morning, stimulating his leg muscles with massage, and lifting weights. Paul Weston was a body man, and he had been given free use of the equipment in the room off the kitchen—equipment Sloan had once used.

Now that she was here, she'd see to it that Paul's duties were increased. She was going to need his help. One of the first things she planned to do was get Sloan Whittaker into his swimming pool whether he wanted to go or not. And for a time she was going to need Paul to get him there.

She had finished reading over the medical reports kept by the previous nurses when Clara came to tell her Mrs. Whittaker had arrived.

Glancing at her watch, Joy raised a speculative brow. "She's early."

"Mrs. Whittaker's anxious to meet you," Clara explained unnecessarily.

The older woman, seated on a long white sofa, was the picture of grace and charm. She was delicate and fine-boned, her hair silver and stylish. She glanced up and smiled when Joy entered the room. Joy watched as the smile died on her lips.

"Miss Nielsen, I can't tell you how pleased I am to meet you," she said with a frown.

"Is something the matter?"

"It's just that I expected someone older," she admitted with quiet concern.

Joy's back remained straight as she sat across from the older woman. "I'm twenty-five," she said in a deliberate, casual tone.

"But Dr. Phelps explained that..." She let the rejoinder fade into silence.

Joy's eyes held the older woman's. "I can assure you that I'm perfectly qualified for the job."

"Oh, my dear, I didn't mean to imply otherwise. It's just that there is so much resting on you. I'm at my wit's end with that son of mine. I've all but given up hope."

"To do so would be premature."

"Have you met Sloan?" Her eyes were anxious.

"This morning."

"And?" she inquired gently.

"And he's bitter, resentful, in pain, mad as hell at the world and everyone in it."

"His last nurse stayed only one day."

"I may not look like much, Mrs. Whittaker," Joy strived to assure the woman, "but I can guarantee it's going to take far more than a few angry words for me to pack my bags."

The woman looked relieved. "I can't tell you how pleased my husband and I are that you agreed to take this assignment. Dr. Phelps has done nothing but rave about you, and quite honestly I don't know how much longer my husband can continue managing the company."

"Pardon?"

Margaret Whittaker lifted the china teacup to her lips and took a sip before continuing. "I'm sorry, dear. I assumed Dr. Phelps told you."

"No, I'm afraid he didn't."

Margaret Whittaker sighed, drawing Joy's rich, brown eyes to the carefully disguised age lines that fanned out from the older woman's eyes and mouth. "My husband came out of retirement after Sloan's accident. I'm afraid the pressure is more than Myron can cope with. We'll be forced to sell the business unless Sloan can assume some of the responsibilities soon."

Joy's face was marred with a thoughtful frown. "I'd like to talk to your husband when it's convenient. I can't make any promises, Mrs. Whittaker, but I would think involving your son in the business again would be in his own best interest."

"Yes, but..." She looked disconcerted, and Joy noted that her hands shook as she replaced the cup to the saucer. "Sloan's convinced he will never walk again. He's given up."

"Mrs. Whittaker, I think you should realize that a man like your son never gives up. Although he wouldn't let you see it, he's fighting. No matter what he says or does."

The silver-haired woman paused, her hands folded primly on her lap. "You're very wise for your years." She regarded Joy thoughtfully. "I apologize for doubting. I can see that you're exactly what Sloan needs."

"I hope I am," she murmured softly, "for your sake."

The soft hum of the wheelchair sounded behind them. Sloan's look was hooded as he moved into the room.

"I wasn't aware you'd arrived, Mother." A sarcastic inflection laced his words.

"I was introducing myself to Miss Nielsen. I hope you appreciate how fortunate we are to get her."

"Oh, yes." His light, mirthless laugh was filled with disdain. "About as lucky as I was the night of the accident."

"Sloan." Margaret Whittaker breathed his name in protest. But his dark head had already turned away, effectively cutting off any further discussion. "You'll have to forgive him." Anger trembled from the sharp edge of his mother's voice.

Joy glanced up, surprised. She would have thought Margaret Whittaker was the type of woman who would never lose her poise. The small display of temper showed Joy how desperate the situation had become for Sloan's mother.

"Don't worry, Mrs. Whittaker. I understand."

An hour later Joy wandered into the kitchen. Clara was busy fixing lunch. "Mr. Whittaker's tray's ready. He has all his meals in his room these days."

"I'll take it to him," Joy volunteered. She wouldn't avoid another confrontation.

She knocked once before swinging open the door. "Good afternoon. I imagine you're anxious for this."

"Then you imagined wrong."

"Listen, big boy, we can do this easy or we can do this hard. The decision is yours."

"Nothing in my life's come easy," he returned sharply.

Joy's laugh was filled with dry challenge. "You're sitting in this showroom house with people fighting to wait on you, and you want my sympathy? You're looking at the wrong woman."

He tipped his head to one side and glared at her. "Get out—or I'll throw you out."

"If you want me to leave, you'll have to do it physically. That's pretty tough for a cripple."

His nostrils flared. "Don't be so confident."

"Oh, I'm sure." She tossed the words at him flippantly. "I run two miles every morning, and in addition to being in great physical condition, I could flatten you with one swift punch. Look at you," she returned smoothly. "You've been sitting in the wheelchair for six months. Your muscles are weak and limp. I doubt that you could lift your own weight. But if you want to try, don't let the fact I'm a woman stop you."

A muscle jumped along the side of his jaw. With a violent shove, he propelled the wheelchair onto the verandah. For now, Joy recognized, he was running; he didn't know what else to do. But the time was fast approaching when he'd have nowhere to go.

Before she left, Joy set up the meal tray. A satisfied smile spread to her eyes as she regarded the meager contents. She'd bet hard cash Sloan Whittaker was going to eat his lunch.

When she returned she noted that she'd been right. He'd devoured every bit and would probably look forward to dinner.

"I'm taking you outside now," she told him in a silky, smooth voice.

"The hell you are."

She didn't argue. Instead she stuck her head out the door and called Paul.

Almost immediately the muscle-bound young man stepped into the room.

"I'd like you to take Mr. Whittaker to the beach."

"No." Sloan shouted savagely.

"Do as I say, Paul," Joy encouraged.

"You so much as touch my chair and you're fired." The way he spoke proved that the threat wasn't an idle one.

"She told me you'd say that."

"Don't do it." The thin line of Sloan's mouth was forbidding.

Uncertain, Paul glanced to Joy for assurance. They'd had a long talk and had reached an understanding where Sloan Whittaker was concerned.

"You can't fire either one of us. You realize that, don't you?" she explained in a bored voice.

"Like hell."

"As I understand the situation, it's your family who hired us, and therefore we work for them. Not you."

Joy could have kissed Paul as he effortlessly pushed Sloan out the bedroom door. Only at rare times had she seen such barely restrained rage. Sloan's handsome face was twisted with it as Paul directed the chair out the back door and onto the sheets of plywood they had laid on the sand to help manipulate his chair.

The day was gorgeous, and a gentle breeze ruffled the soft brown curls about her face.

"Is that all?" Paul looked to her and she nodded, indicating he could leave.

Slipping off her shoes, Joy sat on the soft beach and burrowed her feet in the warm sand. Lifting her face to the soothing rays of the sun, she closed her eyes, oblivious to the angry man beside her.

After several minutes of contented peace, she lowered her gaze and turned to Sloan. He sat erect and angry, like a prisoner of war. He *was* a prisoner in a way, she mused.

"Tomorrow we'll start with the therapy."

"What therapy?" he demanded.

She ignored the censure in his voice. "Your first session will be in the morning with me. I'd thought we'd start in the pool. Later in the afternoon Paul will be helping you tone up the muscles in your arms."

His fingers gripped the arm of his chair with impotent rage. "What has my mother told you?" He breathed the question harshly.

Joy let the sand drain out of her closed fist, watching it bounce against the beach. "Plenty."

"I'll be damned before I fall into your schemes."

"You've already damned yourself, so what difference does it make?" She rose lithely and rolled up the pant legs to her knees. The ocean was several hundred yards away, and she ran down to the water's edge. Her big toe popped the tiny bubbles the surf produced. The sun felt soothing and warm, and she basked in the beauty of the afternoon. When she glanced back she saw that Sloan had somehow managed to turn his chair around and with a determined effort had begun to wheel the chair toward the house.

For now she'd let him escape. His pride demanded as much.

Joy didn't see him again until later that evening. She wasn't surprised when Clara proudly exclaimed that Mr. Whittaker had eaten his dinner.

The sky was pink with the setting sun when she unpacked her flute and stood on the verandah. The music flowed from her unbound and free. There'd been a time Joy had to decide between a musical career and the medical profession. Once the decision had been made she had no regrets. She was a good nurse, and she knew it. Cases like these were her best—

and for a reason. Absently she stopped playing and rubbed her thigh.

"Don't quit."

The words surprised her, and she turned around. Sloan had rolled his chair onto the verandah and was only a few feet from her. Foolishly, Joy hadn't realized their adjacent rooms shared the deck.

Wordlessly she lifted the flute to her lips and played her favorite pieces. Lively jigs followed by the sweet soulful sounds of the classics.

"Where did you ever learn to play like that?" he asked in a whisper.

It was the first time she had heard him speak without being angry. "I started as a child. My father was a musician."

His strong profile was illuminated by the darkening sky. Her eyes fell from the powerful face to the chair, and her heart wanted to cry for him. Arrogant, noble, proud—and trapped.

No. Swiftly she jerked her gaze free. The last thing she wanted was to become emotionally attached to a patient. For now Sloan Whittaker needed her, but that would soon change, and he would be free from the chains that bound him. As he became independent to live and love again, he wouldn't want or need her.

Joy had never fooled herself—she wasn't a beauty. Dark hair and equally dark eyes were probably her best features. Her mouth was too small to be sensuous, her nose a little short, her cheekbones too high. The Sloan Whittakers of this world wouldn't be interested in a hundred-pound misfit.

"Good night, Mr. Whittaker," she spoke softly.

"Miss Nielsen." He remained on the deck while Joy turned sharply and entered her room, closing the sliding-glass door after her. Her heart was pounding wildly, and she placed a calming hand over it. What was the matter with her? Was she becoming attracted to this man? What utter foolishness. Two, maybe three months at the most, and she would be leaving.

Joy woke with the alarm early the next morning. The sun hadn't broken the horizon as she pulled open the drapes and stared into the distance. Quickly she dressed in pants and an old gray sweatshirt. She hadn't run on sand before, and wondered about wearing tennis shoes.

The house was quiet and still as she slipped out the kitchen door. A chill ran goose bumps up her arms, and she jiggled them loosely at her sides as she performed the perfunctory warm-up exercises.

An angry gust of wind nearly staggered her along the beach as the surf pounded the shore. Heedless to the blustery force, Joy picked up her heels and ran. The first quarter-mile was always the hardest. Her lungs heaved with the effort. Sand sank in her shoes, making it almost impossible to maintain her usual pace. Soon she discovered it was much easier if she ran close to the water, where the sand was wet.

When she figured she'd gone a mile or more, she turned and headed back. The house was in sight when she spotted a sea gull walking along the shore dragging its wing. Slowing her pace, she watched as the poor creature pitifully attempted to fly. After several tries the large bird keeled over, exhausted. Realizing the pain it must be enduring, she stopped running hoping she could find some way to help. When she took a tentative step toward it, the gull struggled to sit upright and flee.

Speaking in soothing tones, she fell to her knees in the sand. "Long John Seagull, what are you doing here?"

The bird hobbled a few steps and fell over.

"It looks like you need a friend," she said softly. "Stay here. I'll be right back." With urgent strides, Joy raced toward the house.

Breathlessly, she stumbled into the kitchen.

"Dear heavens, are you all right?" Clara stood with her back to the sink.

Out of wind, all Joy could do was nod.

"You scared me clean out of my skin."

"Sorry." Joy managed the one word. Not wishing to wake Sloan, she moved quietly down the hall to her room. Only yesterday she'd unpacked several emergency medical supplies. She gathered what she thought she'd need in a large shopping bag, found some tough garden gloves, and hurried out of the room.

"You headed for a fire?" Clara asked as Joy scurried through the kitchen a second time.

"No. I found an injured sea gull. I'll be back as soon as I can."

"But, Miss..." Clara called after her.

With the wind beating against her face, Joy ran for all her worth back to her newfound feathered friend.

A half hour later her back ached and her fingers felt swollen and numb with the continued effort of trying to help the bird while not being cut by his powerful beak. As far as she could tell, the wing hadn't been broken, only injured. After carefully applying some antibiotic cream and binding it to his body with a strip of gauze, Joy felt confident the gull would heal.

Long John didn't look pleased when she picked him up and carefully placed him in the sack. A movement out of the corner of her eye captured her attention. She straightened and placed a hand above her eyes to shield them from the glaring sun. She saw that Sloan was on the verandah, watching her. Even from this distance she could see that he was displeased.

"His bark is worse than his bite," Joy informed the bird, who stuck his head out of the sack and looked around. "Don't worry. I know a safe place for you."

Her hair was wet from the shower when Joy came out of her room and closed the door.

"What were you doing this morning?" The question wasn't issued casually but in arrogant challenge.

"Running," she replied, and rotated her gaze to Sloan's face.

He sighed heavily. "I saw you working on something."

"I found a hurt sea gull. His wing," she added. "Are you ready for breakfast?"

Sloan's gaze hardened and shifted to her eyes. "You like to play the role of the rescuer, don't you? Birds, animals, people. Well, get this straight, little Miss Miracle Worker. I don't need you, and furthermore I don't want you. So get out of my life and stay out."

"My, my, we're in a fine mood this morning," Joy said cheerfully. "How do you want your coffee? Lukewarm and in your lap, or perhaps over your head?"

A hint of a smile touched his hard mouth. "Would it be too much to ask for it in a cup?"

"That depends entirely upon you," she chided softly. "Don't go away. I'll be right back."

A few minutes later she brought in his breakfast tray. "You'll be pleased to know I ate in the kitchen,'' she said, a mocking reminder of his earlier statement.

Again a near-smile crossed his face.

"I thought that would please you," she said.

On Joy's instructions Clara had prepared a much lighter meal this morning. A warm croissant was served with butter and homemade strawberry jam. She poured his coffee and set the pot to the side.

"I'll be back in a few minutes with Paul."

"I don't need him this morning," Sloan said stiffly.

"Are you already in your suit?"

"My suit?"

"We're going swimming, remember?"

Sloan laughed coldly. "Like hell."

"It'll probably hurt that much, so prepare yourself."

"Miss Nielsen," he muttered grimly, "there's no way in God's green earth that you're going to get me in that pool, so kindly accept that and save us both a lot of trouble."

"We'll see," she returned lightly.

The grooves around his mouth deepened with defiance. "Has anyone ever told you that you're a stubborn bi—"

"I do find such language unnecessary." She effectively cut him off by pivoting and walking away.

An hour later, dressed in her one-piece turquoise swimsuit, Joy dived into the deep end of the pool. Her slim body sliced through the water. She surfaced and did a couple of laps, enjoying the feel of the cool water against her skin.

When she paused she found Paul standing outside the pool, looking ill at ease and uncertain.

"Whittaker isn't pleased about this."

"I don't imagine he is. If necessary, bring him down here naked. He's coming in this pool one way or another."

"You're sure?"

"Very," she repeated confidently. "Throw him in, if you have to."

"If that's what you want."

Waiting in the shallow end of the pool, Joy could hear Sloan long before seeing him. An angry torrent of abusive words were followed by the sight of a red-faced Paul.

"Thank you, Paul." She smiled her appreciation and glared at Sloan. "The time has come to separate the men from the boys."

Two

A slow smile spread across Joy's face. "Come on in. The water's fine."

"I could hate you for this," Sloan growled.

"I've been hated by better men than you," Joy informed him cheerfully. She didn't doubt Sloan; her job was to channel some of that intensity into the exercises. Clara had told her how much Sloan had loved the pool, swimming laps early every morning. He would again if she had anything to do with it. "Put him in the water, Paul."

She turned and dove into the blue depths, feeling slightly guilty that Paul was left to deal with the abusive end of Sloan's temper. Her turned back offered him the privacy to climb into the water without her seeing Paul lift him. His pride had taken enough of a beating lately, and she didn't want to make this any more difficult than it already was.

When she surfaced at the far end of the pool, Joy noticed Paul was standing back from the pool's edge, his look unsure.

"That'll be all." Treading water, she raised one hand and waved, indicating she wanted him to leave.

Sloan was sitting on the steps that led from the shallow end, his look foreboding. "Let's get this over with so I can get the hell out of here."

"All right," she agreed, swimming toward him. Her arms cut through the water as she stroked. Because of the distance separating them she couldn't hear the savagely muttered words, which was probably just as well.

He held himself rigid, and one hand gripped the side of the pool.

"I've always loved to swim," she announced, and playfully dipped her head back into the cool, aqua-blue water.

Sloan's dark gaze followed her actions.

"When I was a child, my father was the one who taught me," she said. "I loved those days. We could never afford a pool like this, but summer evenings when Dad got off work, my brother, mother, father, and I went swimming in the pool at the park."

Sloan looked bored.

"It seems ironic to me that my father would drown," she continued. Her unflinching gaze met Sloan's. "For a year afterwards I couldn't go near a pool. In some obscure way I think I wanted to punish the water for taking my father."

Sloan exhaled a short, angry breath.

Joy's mouth formed a humorless smile. It'd been a mistake to speak of her beloved father. She couldn't understand why she had—especially with Sloan Whittaker.

"For now all I want you to do is familiarize yourself with the pool. Tomorrow I'm going to start you on a series of exercises. I won't try to kid you. These movements are going to hurt, but they're supposed to."

"Do you want me to leap for joy with some pie in the sky dream you have of my walking again?" His eyes snapped fire.

"No, but I will tell you this. Progress will be slow enough; if you fight me, it'll only take longer."

"In other words, a lot of pain and only a little progress."

"That, Mr. Whittaker, is up to you."

"If it was up to me, you'd get the hell out of my life."

A smile twitched at the edge of her mouth. "I'll be happy to leave, but when I go that wheelchair will be in the attic."

His fist slammed against the water, spraying it along the pool's tiled edge. "Spare me from optimistic women."

"Starting tomorrow, Paul will be taking you to the whirlpool before our session here. There are several reasons for that, none of which would interest you, I'm sure."

His impassive expression didn't alter.

"You can go for now. I'll see you at lunchtime."

"Don't hurry."

The sun's golden rays bathed his pale features. Joy realized that only a year ago Sloan Whittaker would have been bronze and sunbrowned. Once he had been a compellingly handsome man, but pain had chiseled blunted, abrupt lines in his face. His dark eyes seemed to mirror the agony of the past months. Mournful and intense. Joy had seen it before, but never had it affected her like this. In some degree she gave a part of herself to each of her patients. Her greatest fear was that Sloan

Whittaker would take her heart. That she couldn't allow.

"I won't hurry," she answered at last. "I'm not any more anxious to see you than you are me."

"At least we understand one another."

Joy called for Paul and swam laps as the young man helped Sloan out of the water. She was again offering him the privacy that might salvage his pride.

He regarded her skeptically when she brought in his lunch. Later, when she delivered the tray to the kitchen, Joy was pleased to note that he had again eaten a decent meal.

That night, after the sun set, she picked up her flute and stood on the balcony to play. A gentle breeze stirred her hair and felt like a whispered caress against her smooth skin. The sounds of the Beatles' classic, "Yesterday," filled the silence. She loved the song.

Joy paused when she finished, noting that Sloan had rolled onto the balcony and was staring into the still night.

"You can't bring back the past," he said. The words were filled with anger and regret.

"No," she agreed softly, "you can't. Today, this minute. Now, is all that matters."

Again she played the songs she loved best. Anne Murray, Kenny Rogers, mellow sounds that produced a tranquil mood within her.

She sighed as she lowered the musical instrument. The day had been full, and she was exhausted. "Is there anything I can get you before I go inside?" she asked softly, not wanting words to destroy the mood.

At first it didn't appear that he'd heard her. His mouth twisted sardonically and he rotated the wheelchair so that he faced her. "How about new legs, Miss Miracle Worker?"

"I'm fresh out of those," she replied evenly. "I'm afraid you'll have to make do with what you've got."

Joy heard him exhale a frustrated, savage breath and knew her comment hadn't pleased him. With a soft smile she turned away. "Good night, Mr. Whittaker."

He didn't reply, and Joy guessed that he wasn't wishing her anything good.

The next week was miserable, an unceasing confrontation of wills. Sloan fought her every step of the way. Several times it was all she could do not to retaliate out of her own frustration.

She hadn't minced words when she told him the exercises were going to cause him pain, although he never indicated that she was hurting him. He worked with her because he had no choice, and although he didn't resist her as she manipulated his legs, he didn't aid her, either. Some mornings after their session Joy noticed how ashen his face was as he struggled to disguise the agony. The lines of strain were deeply etched about his mouth. He rarely spoke to her, seeming to prefer sullen silence to open confrontation. Apparently he'd learned early that the biting, sarcastic comments rolled off her as easily as the pool water, that she could give as well as she took. In some ways a mutual respect was beginning to blossom, but it didn't lessen the intense dislike he felt for her or the frustration she experienced knowing she wasn't reaching him or gaining his trust. She was failing in the most important area.

Sloan came onto the balcony at night as if waiting for her music. Rarely did he comment, silently wheeling back into his room when she'd finished.

On Saturday Joy rose and dressed at the usual time. Her heart felt weighted, and she wasn't sure why. The crisp morning air felt cool as she slipped out the back door. First she checked Long John, the sea gull she'd found and was nursing. He didn't like the confines of the fenced portion of the yard, but like Sloan he was trapped and unable to flee. The bird squawked and hobbled to the side of the yard when she opened the gate. Several times he had lashed out at her hand, once drawing blood. He didn't trust her, again like Sloan.

For six days she had worked with them both and had failed to earn more than a grudging respect. At least the bird wanted his freedom. But Sloan had no will to walk or enter the mainstream of life. What would make a man content to sit in a chair? Or was this all another battle of their wills, in which he was determined to prove he didn't need her?

Long John squawked, and Joy focused her attention on the bird. "Good morning, fellow," she whispered. "Are you glad to see me?"

The gull stared at her blankly.

"Don't worry, I'm not any more popular with the master, either." She yearned to reach out and comfort her winged friend. She wanted his trust, as she wanted Sloan's, at least enough so that the bird would allow her close enough to touch him. But he wasn't confident enough yet. Moving slowly, she placed a bowl of cut-up fish and high-protein gruel on the ground and filled his bowl with fresh water. On her knees, she held herself motionless for several moments, hoping he would be hungry enough to overcome his natural reserve. It didn't take her long to realize that the bird wouldn't eat as long as she remained.

Releasing the latch, Joy let herself out of the gate and locked it. For a time she stayed and watched, but Long John defiantly remained where he was. The pungent scent of the ocean greeted her as she walked along the shore. A gentle mist wet her face and hair, and she ran a hand along both sides of her cheeks. Tonight she would go out, do something special. She needed to get away. An evening away would give her more perspective.

As she turned and headed back for the house, a solitary figure on the balcony caught her attention. She hesitated, hands thrust deep into jeans pockets. Was Sloan Whittaker watching her? Maybe he was hoping she'd go away and never return.

The morning followed its usual routine. Joy brought him his breakfast.

"Good morning," she greeted with a smile. "You were up bright and early this morning."

His response was muffled and gruff.

"Long John seemed to be in an identical mood this morning."

"Long John what?"

"The sea gull," she explained as she set the tray on the desk.

"Good grief, don't tell me you've still got that poor creature."

"He's improving, which is more than I can say..." She let the rest of what she was going to say fade when Clara appeared in the doorway.

"Mr. Whittaker's here to see you."

"Bring him in, Clara," Sloan instructed briskly.

The older woman shifted from one foot to the other. "Mr. Whittaker said he wanted to talk to Miss Nielsen."

Sloan's gaze swiveled to Joy for a long, considering look. "What could my father possibly have to say to Miss Nielsen?" he demanded harshly.

"I'll take notes, if you'd like," Joy volunteered in a pert tone.

"Don't bother." He drawled his indifference.

Joy felt his gaze burning into her shoulder blades as she stepped out of the room.

Even Clara seemed puzzled that the senior Whittaker wanted to see Joy. The question was in the older woman's eyes as Joy took a left turn into the living room.

"Miss Nielsen." Myron Whittaker stood and extended his hand. He was tall and as large as Margaret Whittaker was petite. His shoulders were as broad as a wrestler's, his hair white and receding from a wide forehead. Joy's hand met his and was clasped firmly.

"My wife mentioned that you would like to speak to me."

"As a matter of fact, yes. I'm glad you've come." She sat in the large modern chair across from the distinguished-looking man. It wasn't hard to tell where Sloan got his compelling features. Father and son were a lot alike.

"It's only fair to tell you how pleased my wife and I are that you've agreed to take on Sloan's case."

"I think I'm the lucky one. I've never had the pleasure of working in such elegant surroundings."

"Yes, well..." The older man cleared his throat. "We want you to know we appreciate what you've done."

"I haven't done anything yet," Joy admitted wryly. "But part of your son's recovery will depend on you."

"Anything." He rubbed a hand across his face, his eyes tired.

"Part of Sloan's therapy will be mental as well as physical. He's got to be brought back into life, given responsibilities." She hesitated and leaned forward slightly so that her elbows rested on her knees. "Your wife mentioned that you've assumed Sloan's job in the company since the accident. In some ways this is good, but the time has come to return those duties."

"How do you mean?"

"Decision-making, paperwork. These are things that can be done from the house. At least come to Sloan when a decision needs to be made. Part of the problem with your son is that he feels useless. Prove to him he's needed."

"He is," Myron returned forcefully.

"Don't overpower him," she suggested. "Start with updates and reports that will keep him in tune with what's happening. Then gradually lead into the other things. I don't know that much about the business, but I'm sure you'll know how to approach this." Dr. Phelps had told her that the Whittakers owned a ski equipment company. Joy had never skied, but from Sloan's home and lifestyle it was easy to see the business had been a profitable one.

Myron Whittaker looked down, but not before his dark eyes conveyed the toll of the last months. "I'm not sure of anything anymore."

"Your son's going to be fine, Mr. Whittaker." She leaned forward and gave the elder Whittaker's clenched fist a reassuring pat. "He's strong-willed and determined."

Tears glistened in the proud man's gaze. He closed his eyes and gripped her hand, lifting it to his lips.

"My, my, isn't this a touching scene." Sloan wheeled into the room. "My nurse? Honestly, Father, I think you're lowering your standards unnecessarily."

Myron Whittaker sprang to his feet, his face twisted with rage. "You will apologize for that remark."

Distraught, Joy's gaze swiveled from father to son. Sloan's hands gripped the wheels of his chair until his knuckles were white. His mouth was slanted and scornful.

"Wheelchair or no wheelchair, I won't have a son of mine make that kind of suggestion."

"Mr. Whittaker, please." Joy could feel the hot color explode in her face. "This isn't necessary."

"It most certainly is," he barked.

How often Joy had heard that same tone of voice. Father and son shared more than looks.

Sloan's hard gaze hadn't relented. "I regret the implication," he managed between clenched teeth.

"If you'll excuse me." Joy all but ran from the room. Her heart felt as if she'd completed a marathon as she let herself into her room. Her hands shook as she slipped into the swimsuit. The decision this morning to get out, go to a movie, anything, had been a good one. Sloan Whittaker was getting to her. Keeping a cool head with this man was essential to success.

When she slipped out of her room and into the hall, she could hear the angry exchange of bitter words. Joy wanted to shout at them both. Arguing would solve nothing. She bit into her bottom lip tightly and moved outside.

Paul was lounging in a chair by the pool when she came out. "Morning," he said. "How's it going?"

Joy rolled her eyes expressively, and Paul laughed. "He's really something, isn't he?"

"You can say that." Her relationship with the other staff members had relaxed considerably. Almost everyone called her Joy. Since she and Paul worked directly with Sloan she felt a certain camaraderie with him, although they rarely had time to talk for more than a few minutes at a time. "How are the afternoon sessions coming?"

Paul shrugged. "Better, I guess. At least he's stopped yelling."

"In other words, he submits, and that's about it."

Paul nodded.

"At least when he yelled we knew he was involved." Absently, Joy slipped off her sandal and dipped her foot in the water. "This lackadaisical attitude concerns me."

"It's like he's given up."

"I won't believe that," Joy murmured thoughtfully. "Not a man like Sloan Whittaker. I think he's afraid to show he cares simply because he cares so much." Joy felt Paul's gaze and glanced up.

"I think you're right."

Joy's look met his. "I'm betting on it."

Clara ambled toward them, wiping her hands on the ever present apron. "Mr. Whittaker told me to say he's ready for you now."

"I'll be right there." Paul sat up and stretched his arms high above his blond head. "See you in a few minutes."

"I'll be ready." Joy waited until he was out of view before dropping the terry cloth cover and stepping into the water. It gently lapped against her waist. Lowering her lashes, she laid back, paddling her hands at her side to keep afloat. Even with her ears in the water she heard the approach of Sloan's chair. But she remained as she was until certain Sloan was in the water.

As she straightened, their eyes met and clashed across the distance of the pool. Her attention was diverted by Paul, who waved.

"See you later, Joy."

"Joy?" Sloan spit out the word distaste-fully. "Your name is Joy?"

She wouldn't rise to the barbed comment.

"Talk about irony." His laugh lacked warmth. "A torturer named Joy. It's almost hysterical."

Little he could say or do would intimidate her. She'd done verbal battle with him too of-ten to fall prey to another needless confronta-tion.

"Are you ready?"

"No, I'm not." He held himself stiffly against the side of the pool. One elbow was el-evated onto the tile rim, supporting his weight.

Undeterred, Joy swam to his side. Viciously he lunged for her, his fingers biting punish-ingly into her upper arm.

She attempted to shrug free, but his hold was surprisingly strong.

"I hope it hurts," he said cruelly.

"Let go."

"What do you know of pain?" he sneered. "How can you possibly know what it is to lie in a hospital and pray to God you'll die just so the agony stops?"

With her jaw clenched, Joy tried to pry his fingers loose. Already she could imagine a bruise forming.

Sloan tightened his grip. ''What could you know of pitying looks and lost dreams?''

She struggled, and demanded a second time, ''Let me go.''

''Does it hurt? Good, it's supposed to.'' His eyes darkened with emotion. ''Be objective about it. Isn't that what you said to me? Your turn, Miss Miracle Worker.''

Boldly she met his gaze, and to her horror tears welled, blurring her vision. She hadn't expected to cry, and hated herself for the weakness. Burying her chin in her neck, she took in a shuddering breath.

His hand relaxed, setting her free. As she pulled away she heard him utter a frustrated groan. Twisting her upper torso, she dove under the surface. The water felt cool against the flushed skin of her face. When she thought her lungs would burst, she surfaced and found herself at the far end of the pool. An angry bruise had turned her skin black and blue. Her arm throbbed.

"Paul," Sloan shouted. The muscle-bound man appeared almost immediately. "Get me out of here," he muttered thickly.

Paul glanced at Joy, who nodded and turned her back to the pair. A hot tear scalded her cheek. What did she know about pain? It was funny enough to make her want to laugh.

Purposely she avoided Sloan at lunchtime. Clara took his meal in to him and returned with a worried frown. "Didn't so much as touch it. His favorite soup, mind you."

Alone at the kitchen table, Joy released a broken sigh.

"And you're no better," Clara accused. "You've done nothing more than rearrange the food on your plate. What's going on around here?"

"I guess it's an off day. Everyone's entitled to those now and then."

"Off day?" Clara clucked. "The air around here feels like an electrical storm passed through. And Mr. Whittaker and his son fighting? I don't know when that's happened." She wiped a hand across her wrinkled brow, her look narrow with question. "And you look like you've lost your best friend."

Joy gave the older woman a weak smile. "You're right," she said with determination. "I need a change of pace. Don't fix dinner for me tonight. I'm going out."

"I'd say it's about time." Clara nodded approvingly. "Pretty young thing like you should be dancing every night."

Joy laughed. Young she couldn't deny, but pretty was something else again.

She wouldn't be able to avoid Sloan forever, but she gladly relinquished her duties that afternoon. Without explanation, Paul seemed to know she needed the break. When she took part of the day off to go shopping, no one questioned her. At the time she was hired, the Whittakers had told her to set her own hours.

Although Joy browsed around several shops, she didn't buy anything. It felt good to get away, if only for a few hours. She checked the newspaper and drank coffee in a small cafe. A couple of movies she wanted to see were playing, and Joy decided to take one in later.

Clara was busy in the kitchen peeling apples when Joy returned.

"Did you enjoy yourself?"

"It was nice," Joy admitted, and handed the woman one long-stemmed rose. "This is for you."

"Joy." She took the flower and sniffed it appreciatively. "What are you doing buying me flowers?"

"Well, actually, I didn't buy it," Joy admitted grudgingly. "I picked it from the bush outside."

Clara laughed and gave her a spontaneous hug. "I knew the minute I saw you what a dear girl you are."

Joy sat on the countertop, dangling her feet over the edge and talking to Clara for several minutes. She had the impression Clara wouldn't allow many the privilege of invading her home territory so freely. She stayed in the kitchen until dinner was almost ready.

Luxuriating in a bubble bath, she hoped to wash away some of the unpleasantness of the day. A smile touched her face. Could one ever wash away hurts and pains? Dear heavens, she was becoming philosophical.

The sky was painted a bold shade of pink, and Joy paused to admire the vibrant color as she slipped a full-length short-sleeved housecoat over her head.

How could the night be so beautiful when the day had been so ugly? Joy mused. Without thought, she wandered onto the balcony. The palms of her hands rested against the painted rail.

"Lovely, isn't it?"

Joy froze.

"Sometimes when I sit here and stare into the sunset, I can almost forget." The whispered words were spoken so softly that Joy had to strain to hear.

The sound of Sloan's chair told her he was coming toward her. She didn't move.

A finger traced the pattern of the ugly bruise on her arm. "Did I do that?"

"Yes," she answered without turning.

"Dear Lord," he muttered, his voice suddenly thick. "You must hate me."

"No," she replied softly, and turned her face to him. "I don't."

Again he ran his index finger along the bruise. His touch was gentle, almost a caress, as if he wanted to blot out the pain he had caused.

"I'm going out for a while tonight," she announced.

He stiffened and dropped his hand. "A date?"

"No." She shook her head. "Just a movie. I'm going alone."

His hands rolled the chair back a couple of feet, then swiveled it around, presenting her a view of his back. "Have a good time, Joy."

A frown drove creases into her brow. "Thank you."

He hesitated a second before wheeling into his room.

Joy watched him go. Sloan regretted the incident this morning with his father and later with her in the pool. He was a man driven to the limits of his endurance. Mentally, Joy pictured him standing at a crossroads. He would either choose life or a living death. Unconsciously she brushed the hair off her forehead as a smile played over her face. Interestingly, she had viewed him standing, and not in a wheelchair. Why such a nonsensical thing should lighten her spirits she didn't know.

Joy was whistling on her way out the front door. She hadn't been hungry and had skipped dinner. All of a sudden she felt ravenous. There wasn't time to stop and get something before the movie, so she decided to wait until after.

The show was a light comedy that made her laugh, and heaven knew she was in the mood to smile.

On the way down the coast highway, Joy pulled off at a fast-food restaurant. She hadn't paid much attention to the kind of food until she stepped out of the car. Fish. The tantalizing aroma of deep-fried fish and crisp potatoes filled the air.

Joy read over the menu and absently wondered if Sloan knew about this place. He would have, of course, since it was only a few miles from the house. But how long had it been since he'd tasted something like this?

"Can I help you?" An eager-faced youth leaned halfway out the order window.

"Yes." Joy's eyes didn't leave the menu that was painted in bold-faced letters over the grill. "I'd like a double order of fish-and-chips. And a Pepsi."

"Will that be all?"

"No, make that two orders," she added impulsively.

"To go?"

"Pardon?" Joy's puzzled gaze found the girl's.

"Do you want to eat here or take out?" she asked in an impatient breath.

"Take out."

Even as she paid for the meal, Joy wondered what had possessed her to do anything so foolish. No use lying to herself—she'd bought the second fish order for Sloan.

The lights to his room weren't visible from the front of the house. Joy carried the grease-stained white sack into her bedroom and immediately went out onto the balcony.

His drapes were open, but the room was dark. He often sat alone with the lights off. Sometimes she thought he preferred it like that. He could hide in the shadows, but not in the light.

Tentatively she knocked on the sliding-glass door and opened it just a crack.

Silence.

"Are you awake?" She whispered the question, not wishing to disturb him if he happened to be asleep. Her eyes adjusted to the dim interior and searched the room. He sat in the corner, his chin propped up by his fist.

"How was the movie?"

"Great."

His chuckle was filled with quiet humor. 'Why are we whispering?"

"I don't know." She laughed and slid open the door. "I didn't have dinner, so I stopped off at a fish-and-chips place up the road."

"Not Mobey Jake's?"

"I didn't notice the name, but it had a neon whale flashing off and on."

"That's the one. The food's terrific."

"I brought you an order back too."

An uncomfortable pause followed her announcement. "Isn't that fraternizing with the enemy?"

"Could be," she agreed with a secret smile. "But my mother once told me I'd catch a lot more flies with honey than vinegar. But then, my mother never met you."

Three

A contented feeling moved through Joy as she sat up in bed and stretched. Linking her fingers high above her head, she arched her back and released a long, drawn-out yawn.

She couldn't remember an evening she enjoyed more than the one spent with Sloan. He had chuckled when she relayed the movie plot and the antics of the characters. It was the first time Joy had heard the sound of his laughter. The feeling it had produced was warm and pleasant. She had seen him grit his teeth and muffle groans as she manipulated his legs, but never his amusement. How much more she preferred dark eyes that crinkled with laugh lines to ones that struggled to disguise pain.

She dressed in jeans and a loose-fitting T-shirt. Some of the fish fillets had been left over, and she wanted to see if Long John would eat out of her hand. Great strides seemed to have been made with Sloan, and she was eager to see if the injured gull was also any more wiling to accept her as his friend.

"Good morning, L.J.," she greeted as she let herself into the yard. The gate latched behind her as she stepped to the food bowl and bent down extending her hand. "See what I've got here? Fish," she answered her own question in reassuring tones. "And I happen to know gulls are particularly fond of fish. I'm not so sure about fried fish, but I think you ought to give it a try."

With an ambling gait that reminded her of Clara Barnes, the bird took a step in her direction.

"Obviously you've got keen eyesight," Joy encouraged her feathered friend.

When the bird was only a few inches away, she edged closer, wanting him to take the fish from her. Almost immediately Joy realized her mistake. The razor-sharp beak slicked into the back of her hand instead of the food. Blood gushed from the open cut. Inhaling a sharp breath, Joy dropped the fish and jerked upright. In a protective movement she held her hand to her body and hurried out the gate. Blood seemed to be everywhere. The gull had apparently sliced into a vein. The pain was sharp as she quickly stepped back into the house. Clara wasn't in the kitchen. Joy was grateful she didn't have to make unnecessary explanations. From the flow of blood, it looked as if she might need a suture or two.

Intent on escaping unseen into her bedroom, Joy nearly stumbled over Sloan, who was wheeling down the wide hallway.

"Joy, why the rush?"

"I'm sorry," she mumbled, pressing her hand to her shirt. "I didn't mean to startle you."

"You're hurt."

Sloan's pallor became sickly. He swallowed and narrowed his gaze on her hand.

"I'm fine."

"You need a doctor."

"What I need is to see how deep this is."

Stepping into her room, she moved directly to the bathroom sink and held her cut hand under a slow faucet. In the background she could hear Sloan yelling for Clara. Within moments the red-faced cook came rushing into the room.

"I got cut. It's no major catastrophe. Darn, it looks like it may need to be sewn up." Angry at herself for her own stupidity, Joy felt like stamping her foot and yelling. Didn't she know better than to rush something as delicate as trust? As an injured bird, she would have probably reacted the same way.

"I'll get Paul to drive you to the hospital." With agitated, worried movements, Clara rushed out of the room.

The fuss everyone was making didn't lessen Joy's feelings of self-reproach. A small towel was wrapped around her right fist and held protectively against her stomach. Joy grabbed her purse off the dresser, fumbled with the clasp, and took out her car keys.

Sloan was gone, but she could hear him speaking to someone on the phone. His voice was angry and urgent. Footsteps could be heard rushing up the stairs.

"What happened?" Paul directed the question to Joy.

"I got cut. It's my own stupid fault. But it looks like I'm going to need a few sutures. A vein's been sliced."

A pale Sloan rolled his chair from his room. "Dr. Phelps is on his way."

"Dr. Phelps," Joy repeated, aghast. "You didn't call him, did you?" The whole situation was quickly becoming ridiculous, she thought. "You don't ask a noted surgeon to make a house call for a few stitches," she shouted sharply.

"Paul," Sloan shouted, no less calm, "get her into my room."

With a supportive hand under her elbow, Paul led her into Sloan's quarters.

"This is ridiculous," she hissed under her breath.

Sloan wheeled in after her. "Sit her in my chair."

"I might get blood on it," she protested.

"For once, just once," Sloan ground out between clenched teeth, "will you do as I ask?"

Pinching her mouth tightly shut, Joy plopped down on the expensive leather recliner. Paul hovered over her and Sloan rolled his chair back and forth across the room.

"For heaven's sake, you two look like you expect me to keel over dead any minute." Her wit didn't please Sloan, who tossed her a fiery glare. "Look at you." She directed her words to Sloan. "You're absolutely pale. Do you mean to tell me that after everything you've gone through you can't stand the sight of blood?"

"Shut up, Neilsen." The authority in his voice brooked no resistance.

"Well, for heaven's sake, would you stop doing that. You're making me nervous."

"Doing what?"

"That." She pointed her finger at his chair. "You've got to be the only man in the world, who paces in a wheelchair."

Paul chuckled, and she tipped her head back and rolled her eyes expressively. "How could you have phoned Dr. Phelps?" she asked, and groaned with embarrassment.

"You've lost a lot of blood." His voice pounded like thunder around the room.

"I'm fine," she nearly shouted, and bounded to her feet, stalking to the far side of the room. Her angry glare met Sloan's as they stared at one another, the distance of the room separating them.

"How'd it happen?" Paul inserted, apparently in an attempt to cool tempers.

"It was my own stupid fault." She watched as Sloan's hands tightened around the arms of his chair in a strangling hold. "I tried to get L.J. to eat out of my hand . . ."

"L.J.?" Sloan interrupted.

"The sea gull I found."

"She named him Long John," Paul explained with a trace of humor. "Rather appropriate, I thought."

"I didn't ask what you thought." Sloan's mouth twisted sarcastically. "I want that bird destroyed."

"No." Joy's voice trembled with rage. "You can't kill something because it was protecting itself. I told you, the whole thing was my fault."

"I don't want the sea gull around," Sloan shouted.

"Then I'll find someplace else."

The air between them was as cold as an arctic blast.

Paul moved to the center of the room. "Interestingly enough, I happened to read the other day that there aren't such things as sea gulls. Kittiwakes, black-backed gulls, and herring gulls, but technically there are no sea gulls."

Speechless, Joy stared blankly at her muscular friend until she recognized that he was placing himself between her and Sloan, granting them each the space to cool their tempers.

Clara could be heard fussing in the hall. "This way, Dr. Phelps."

Everyone's attention was centered on the door as the tall, dark-haired doctor entered the room.

"Dr. Phelps," Joy began, "I'm so embarrassed."

"Anyone that lets a stupid bird slash their hand in two deserves to be," Sloan inserted dryly.

Joy darted him a warning glance.

"Now that I'm here, I might as well have a look." Professional and calm, Dr. Phelps set his black bag on the desk and hung his light coat over the back of the chair.

"And since you're here, it might do well to check Mr. Whittaker. I'm sure he's due for an enema or something."

The good doctor chuckled as he removed the towel from her hand. A fresh supply of blood oozed from the laceration as he pried it gently with his fingers. "Nothing a couple of sutures won't cure," he murmured thoughtfully.

"I have most of the supplies you'll need in my room," she told him, and stood, leading the way.

The necessary equipment was laid out across the small tabletop as Dr. Phelps injected the topical anesthetic. Nonplussed, Joy watched him work. Having seen this so many times in the past, it amazed her how unaffected she could remain when it was her own hand.

The dull ache continued after he bandaged the hand in white gauze.

"How's it going with Sloan?" he asked as he worked. They'd only talked briefly one time since she'd taken over the assignment.

"I'm not sure," she answered honestly. "I'm beginning to think some progress is being made, but it's too soon to tell."

"I don't know of anyone else who could reach him." The compassionate grey eyes searched hers. "Have you told him yet?"

"No, but he'll see soon enough."

The dark head bobbed in agreement. "If you have any problems, don't hesitate to call me."

"I won't."

"And listen, it might not be a bad idea to keep this hand out of the water a couple of days."

She laughed softly. "Sloan will love that."

"Speaking of the man, I meant to check him, since I'm here." He discarded the items he'd used and closed his bag. "I'll give you a call later in the week."

"Thank you, Doctor."

"I'm glad to finally be in your debt. You're the one who continues to save me." The good-natured smile left his face as he noted her hand. "Go ahead and remove those sutures yourself in a week or so. Use your own judgment."

Dr. Phelps left a few moments later and Joy laid back against her pillow, intent on resting her eyes a few minutes. Before she was aware of it, it was afternoon and she'd been asleep for hours.

A blanket had been laid over her, and she recognized it as one from Sloan's room. How had he gotten in? The door to his quarters had been widened to accommodate the wheelchair, but hers hadn't. A gentle breeze ruffled the closed drapes, and she realized the sliding-glass door had been left open.

What a puzzling man Sloan Whittaker was. Rubbing the sleep from her eyes, Joy sat up and swung her short legs off the mattress. Already, half the day had been wasted.

Someone knocked softly on her bedroom door.

"Come in," Joy called.

Clara opened the door and came in carrying a large tray. "I thought you might like something to eat."

"But you didn't need to bring it to me," Joy protested. "I'm not incapacitated, you know."

"Mr. Whittaker insisted that you take the rest of the day off. You rest and I'll bring in your meals."

"But, Clara, that's ridiculous."

"Mr. Whittaker was real worried about you. I can't remember a time he acted like this."

Leaning against the pillows the cook had fluffed up against the headboard, Joy laughed. "For all his bark, our Mr. Whittaker is a marshmallow. Did you see how pale he got when he saw the blood on my shirt? For a minute I was afraid he was going to pass out."

Clara's look was thoughtful. "Mr. Whittaker doesn't like the sight of blood. At least not since the accident."

The humor drained out of Joy's eyes. She was being callous. Of course the blood had bothered him, especially since he'd lain helplessly in a pool of his own.

The lack of sensitivity robbed Joy of her appetite. She made a token attempt to eat so as not to arouse Clara's suspicions and tucked a few items inside a napkin to give L.J.

After changing into a clean blouse for the third time that day, Joy carried the half-empty tray into the kitchen. "Thanks, Clara. Lunch was delicious."

"Since you're up, I think Mr. Whittaker would like to talk to you. He's in his room."

"Sure," she agreed, and swallowed tightly.

With the blanket clenched to her breast, Joy tapped lightly on Sloan's door and waited for his answer before entering.

They eyed one another warily. "You wanted to see me?"

"Not particularly," Sloan snapped.

Shrugging off his gruff welcome, she laid the blanket at the foot of the bed and turned with forced calm. "I'll see you later. By the way..." She hesitated, her back to him. "Thank you for putting the blanket over me."

"I didn't."

Joy frowned curiously. He was lying, and she didn't know why. Later, as she walked along the windswept shore, Joy guessed that he didn't want her to know he was concerned.

Paul saw her and waved as she climbed atop a sand dune. Joy raised her good hand and returned the gesture. It was another gorgeous April afternoon. How quickly she was coming to love this beach, this house, this... Her mind refused to form "man." So much of herself was tied up with this case: her skill, her ego, the almost desperate desire to help lift him from the mire of self-pity. The dangers were clear, but as long as she was aware and protected herself, she would be safe.

With long-legged strides, Paul raced to her, feet kicking up sand as he ran.

"How do you feel?" she queried.

"Great."

"Feel up to another confrontation with the master?" she asked in a teasing voice.

"Naw, it's much more fun watching you two argue. But since you're a bit under the weather, what would you like?"

"You've still got that plywood around, haven't you? Let's get him down here on the beach."

"He isn't going to like it," Paul warned.

"Heavens, so what's new? Sloan Whittaker doesn't like anything."

Together they laid down the thick boards of wood. Paul insisted on wheeling Sloan down, and Joy didn't argue. She didn't feel like arguing with Sloan, not today. Her hand throbbed; foolishly she'd refused anything for pain when Dr. Phelps asked. Sitting and soaking up the sun sounded far more appealing than a verbal battle with Sloan.

"I suppose this was your idea, Nielsen," Sloan ground out as Paul pushed the chair down the wooden planks.

She pretended the wind had blown the words away by cupping a hand over her ear.

"You heard me."

"Well, damn it if I didn't."

Paul glanced from one to the other and chuckled. "He's all yours. Let me know when you need me."

"Thanks, Paul." She smiled her thanks and watched as he turned and headed back to the house.

"You enjoy doing this, don't you?"

"Doing what?"

"This kind of garbage!" He hurled the words at her savagely, as if venting his anger would lessen his confusion. "You seem to have the mistaken impression that once thrust into the beauty of nature I'll forget all my troubles and thank God for the gift of life."

"No." She sat in the sand beside him, her bare toe burrowing under the granules. "I thought a little sun might add color to your face."

"You're lying."

"If you say so," she agreed pleasantly, tilting her face upward and coveting the golden rays. "You know, Whittaker, if you didn't work so hard at disliking this, you could come to enjoy it."

"Never."

"Want me to bury your feet in the sand?"

"No," he hissed.

"Then be quiet. You're destroying my peace."

"Good. I haven't had a peaceful moment from the day you arrived."

She ignored him, pretending not to hear his movements.

"Nielsen."

Opening her eyes, she quirked her head inquiringly. Sloan dumped his sweater over her head. "That's what I think of your loony ideas."

"For a cripple, you're mighty brave."

"And you're a sad excuse for a woman. Don't you wear anything but pants? What's the matter, are you afraid to let a man see your legs?"

"Legs," she cried dramatically. "You want legs, I'll give you legs." Rolling to her feet, she pulled up her pants to her knees and pranced around like a restless filly. The sight of Paul escorting a tall blonde halted Joy in mid-stride. Stopping completely, her hands fell lifelessly to her side and she took a huge breath. "It looks like you've got company."

"Company?" Sloan barked. "I don't want to see anyone. Send them away."

"It's too late for that." A bitter taste filled her mouth. Joy would have killed for a figure like this blonde's. Tall. Willowy. Every brick stacked in the right place. And a face that would stop traffic.

As the two drew closer, the woman's pace increased. "Oh, my darling, Sloan. No one told me. Oh, Sloan." She fell to her knees and buried her perfectly shaped head in his lap. The delicate shoulders shook with sobs.

Sloan's hand lifted, hesitated, then finally patted the blonde's back.

Joy took a step in retreat, not wishing to be a witness to this scene. Sloan's eyes found Joy's and cast her an unmistakable look of appeal.

"I'll leave you two alone."

"No," Sloan barked, his intense gaze demanding that she stay.

"Maybe you'd enjoy some iced tea? I'll be back in a jiffy."

"Nielsen?" Sloan's low voice threatened.

"I'll be right back." Wickedly she fluttered her long lashes at him.

Paul carried a lounge chair for her while Joy managed the tray with two tall glasses of fresh iced tea each with a slice of lemon attached to the side.

Apparently the blonde had composed herself. Dabbing her eyes with a scented hankie, she stood at Sloan's side, her blue eyes filled with compassion and sweetness.

"I'm afraid Trixie can't stay," Sloan announced, and his gaze narrowed menacingly on Joy. "Paul, would you kindly escort her to her car?"

In true gentlemanly fashion, Paul placed his arm around the blonde's shoulders and whis-

pered comforting words to her as he walked
her toward the house.

"Neilsen, you do that to me again and
I'll—"

"Do what?" she inquired innocently.

His hand sliced the air dramatically.
"Couldn't you have done something? I
thought you were my self-appointed rescuer.
Well, rescue me! The minute I really need
you—off you fly with the excuse of getting
iced tea."

"What in the Sam Hill did you expect me to
do?"

"I don't know. That's your job, isn't it?"

"No," she snapped back, then started to
laugh.

"What's so funny?" he demanded.

"You! Think about it. It's a sad commentary on your life when you want me to rescue
you from the arms of a beautiful woman."

A poor facsimile of a smile touched his
mouth. "Couldn't you see she was throwing
herself all over me, oozing pity?"

"Women like to cry," she explained pa-
tiently, and sat down in the sand cross-legged.
She took a tall glass and handed him the other.
"It gives us a reason to appear feminine."

"And Trixie knows how good she looks with tears clinging to her lashes. Her big, blue eyes staring into mine."

"You sound like you've made lots of women cry."

"Hundreds," he returned sarcastically.

"I wouldn't doubt it." Joy laughed lightly.

"What about you?"

"I don't know of any women who've cried over me," she teased, the wind blowing her soft brown curls across her high cheekbones.

"You know what I mean."

Staring in her tea, she shrugged lightly. "Only one."

"Who?"

Joy swallowed around the tight lump that formed in her throat. "My father."

They were silent after that.

"Tell me about your family." Sloan said after a long time.

"My father was a senior high music teacher and band director, my mother a housewife. There's only my brother. He's two years older, lives in Santa Barbara, has a wife and two children."

"Is he as gutsy as you?"

"Doug? Yes, only in a different way. He's a policeman."

"You said your father drowned." The words were issued softly. His voice inflection made it a question.

Arms wrapped around her knees, she stared out at the waves gently lapping the shore. "He died in Mexico, three summers ago. Mom and Dad flew down to celebrate their anniversary. Two little boys, about eight and ten, tourists from Texas, got trapped in the undertow." She paused, reliving the horror of that summer again. "Dad managed to save one. He died with his arms around the ten-year-old. My mother looked on from the beach helpless." Even blandly stating the facts brought tears to her eyes, and she touched her forehead to her knee, not wishing him to witness her emotion. Once her breathing had returned to normal, she lifted her head. "My father was a wonderful man."

"I already knew that," Sloan murmured, and, reaching out a hand, lightly stroked her hair. His touch was gentle. Joy hadn't expected his comfort and expelled a whispering sigh at the warm sensation that cascaded over her from the touch of his hand to her head.

"What about you?" she asked to purposely change the subject.

"There's only me. I think my parents wanted more, but mother had a difficult pregnancy and the doctors advised her not to."

"Were you always..."

"Rich?" he finished for her.

"That's not the word I would have used, but yes."

"The company's been in the family for three generations. This summer house is a new acquisition."

"This is your summer home?" Her gaze flew over her shoulder to the magnificent structure behind her. The idea that it was a summer home shocked her. This was the sort of place anyone would dream about living in all year long.

"Usually I live in a condo in Palm Springs, but I have apartments in Switzerland and New York. Had," he corrected on a bitter note.

Her mouth dropped open and she widened her eyes and swallowed. "Oh."

"For heaven's sake, don't go all goo-goo-eyed on me."

Joy forced her mouth closed.

"Actually, this house belongs to my parents. Does that make you feel any less intimidated?"

"Yes." She gestured weakly with her hand. "Sure."

"Does that shocked look mean I'm going to get a little respect?"

"No." She shook her head emphatically. "It means I'm asking for a raise. I hope you realize I'm still paying off a government loan for my college education."

He chuckled then. The rich, clear sounds were carried with the wind. Joy tossed her head back and smiled at him. This moment was one she would treasure when it came time for her to go; Joy was sure of it. The sun. The sand. The sea. And the sound of Sloan's full laugh.

Jumping to her feet, she took off toward the sea.

"Hey, where are you going?" He called after her, his brow creased in thick lines.

"To look for seashells." Swinging her hands high at her side, she walked backwards, taunting him. "Want to come?"

"Yes!" he shouted, surprising her. "Bring one of those pieces of wood forward. Once the chair gets on wet sand, you can push me."

"Push you?" Her laugh was musical. "Wheel yourself, bub."

His dark eyes sparkled. "All right, lazy. I'll do the heavy work."

Joy did as he suggested, dragging the wood around until they managed to manipulate the chair close to the shore.

"Come on, I'll race you."

Sloan quirked his mouth to one side. "Trying to take advantage of a cripple, are you?"

"I was going to even the odds," she added with an offended look.

"Sure you were."

"No, honest." She crossed her heart with her index finger and burst into peals of laughter at the look on his face. "Okay, okay, I'll run backwards."

"And hop on one foot?"

"No. That's too much."

"All right. On your mark, get ready, go," Sloan shouted.

Joy paused, hands on her hips, looking on helplessly. His arms worked furiously as he rotated the large wheels.

"Hey, I wasn't ready," she shouted at him.

"Tough." The wind brought the lone word back to her. She watched as the muscles of his upper arms flexed with the effort.

Serious now, Joy turned around and began to jog backwards. Within a minute she was even with him. "Let's negotiate," she protested, gasping for breath.

"Do you concede?"

"Anything."

Sloan stopped and swiveled the chair around so that he faced her.

Soft laughter rose within her, and until she regained her breath Joy leaned forward and rested her hands on her knees. "You cheated," she chided him. "I wasn't ready."

"You looked ready to me."

Her back was to the ocean, and she heard Sloan's shout of warning just as the wave crashed against her legs, hitting the back of her thighs.

Sloan dissolved into fits of laughter at the shocked look that came over her face.

"You did that on purpose," she gasped in outrage.

"I didn't, I swear it."

Flinging her hand forward, she managed to catch enough water to spatter him with a few drops. Not to be deterred, she waited until the next big wave came in and scooped as much water as her cupped hands would hold. Giggling and breathless, she ran toward him, stumbled, and fell forward.

In split-second response, Sloan reached out to catch her, breaking the impact of the fall. But to her horror, Joy pulled him out of the wheelchair and took him with her to the ground.

He lay partially on top of her. "Joy." His voice was urgent. "Are you alright?"

"Disgraced, but otherwise unruffled. And you?" Her back was pressed against the rough sand.

He didn't answer her. Their eyes met, and a flood of warmth swept through her. The laughter was gone from his gaze, and she stared back wordlessly, almost afraid to breathe. Joy knew she should break away, do something, anything, to stop what was happening. But the hunger in his look held her motionless. She didn't blink.

Slowly he lowered his head, blocking out the sunlight. Their breaths mingled as his lips hovered a hair's space above her own. No longer could she see his face. Her heart was crying out to him, begging him to stop and at the same time pleading with him to kiss her. It was no use fighting her clamoring sensations, and she closed her eyes.

Very gently, as if in slow motion, Sloan fit his mouth over hers. At first his lips barely skimmed the surface, as if he didn't want this but couldn't help himself.

But when Joy slid her hands around his neck, his mouth crushed hers, forcing her lips to part. Fiercely he wrapped his arms around her, half lifting her from the sand.

Abruptly he released her and rolled to the side so that they lay next to one another on their backs. Joy felt the cold air and kept her eyes closed. She shouldn't have let this happen. It could possibly undermine everything she had struggled to build in this relationship.

"You asked for that," he said bitterly. "You've been asking for it all day. Are you satisfied now? How does it feel to be kissed by a cripple? Or is this one of the extra services you provide for all your patients?"

Four

"**M**r. Whittaker's breakfast is ready," Clara announced as she set the tray on the kitchen counter. The older woman studied Joy. "You want me to take it in to him?"

For a moment the offer was tempting. But Joy couldn't. Sloan would know why, and he must never guess the effect his kiss had had on her. How stupid she'd been to have let it happen. Now she must pay for her foolishness.

"Air's been a mite thick between you two," Clara mumbled as she set a pan in the sink and filled it with tap water.

"What do you mean?" Joy glanced up guiltily.

"I don't suppose you'd think ol' Clara would notice. But things got real quiet after you and Mr. Whittaker was on the beach yesterday. Mr. Whittaker didn't eat no dinner. You didn't eat no dinner. And then you didn't play that clarinet the way you done at nights lately.''

"Flute," Joy corrected. "You're right. I didn't play. My... my hand was hurting.''

Unconcerned, Clara hummed a soft tune. "You want me to take him breakfast?''

"No," she said with a forced smile. "I'll do it.''

Balancing the tray on her knee, Joy knocked loudly on Sloan's door twice. Purposely she'd avoided him the remainder of the day, hoping that if she put at some distance what had happened on the beach they could both look at it in perspective. But the nagging questions persisted. How could anything that felt so good, so right, be a fluke, a mistake?

"Come in," Sloan growled.

Forcing a smile on her mouth, Joy opened the door. "I can see you're in your usual good mood this morning.''

"What's so wonderful about it?" Sloan demanded irritably, and pivoted his chair around so that he faced her. "It's just like any other morning for a cripple.''

"You're not a cripple." Her eyes focused away from him as she placed the tray on the desk.

His laugh was short and derisive. "But isn't that what you're so fond of calling me?"

Joy inhaled a calming breath. "I call you one to get a rise out of you. You're a smart man; I'd have thought you had that figured out by now."

"Not many men I know roll around in one of these things," he challenged, and his hand patted the large wheel of his chair.

"It's true that you and that chair are constant companions." Joy wasn't going to argue with him. "But in your mind you're running free."

"How do you know what's in my mind?" he protested, his eyes darkening.

"In some ways it's not so difficult," she returned thoughtfully, her back to him.

"Oh?" Again his voice was thick with challenge.

"What is this? An interrogation?" Joy whirled around and leaned against the desk, her hands behind her. "Remember, it's Monday morning. You'll have to make allowances for me on Mondays. It takes my heart ten minutes to start beating once I crawl out of bed."

"You ran this morning."

Joy turned around and lifted the silver warming dome off the breakfast plate and set it aside. "How'd you know that?"

"I watched you."

"Oh." It was crazy, the effect the information had on Joy. Her hands felt clammy and her face warm. She didn't want him invading her life this way. When the time came for her to leave, it would only make things more difficult. And when she left, Joy vowed, she would walk away from Sloan Whittaker intact. Whole. She wouldn't leave this man her heart.

"What's that?" Sloan's words cut into her musings.

"What's what?"

"That." He pointed to the breakfast tray.

"Oatmeal, toast, and juice." She looked at him with a blank stare.

"I hate oatmeal."

"Rolled oats are good for you," she countered with a smile.

"Yes, but have you ever asked yourself what they rolled them with?"

"No," she admitted with a small laugh, "I can't say that I have. Do you want me to have Clara cook you something else?"

He looked up at her, his eyes wide and disbelieving. "Neilsen, you're mellowing."

Joy's nerves suddenly felt threadbare. The need to escape was overpowering. "Maybe I am," she agreed. "But don't count on it," she murmured, and made her exit from the room.

Her hands were trembling as she leaned against the wall in the hallway. She needed its support. With a determined lift of her chin, she straightened and returned to the kitchen. This wasn't like her, but there seemed to be a lot of things she didn't understand about herself anymore.

"Problems?" Clara questioned, her large brown eyes watching Joy with concern.

"None. Why?"

Clara's look was disconcerting. The older woman was too observant not to notice the high color of Joy's flushed cheeks.

"You need to talk to ol' Clara?"

"No, I'm fine," Joy dismissed the offer. "But thanks anyway."

"Any time, child. Any time."

The sounds of Clara humming followed Joy down the hallway to her room. The door clicked, and she walked across the room to stand in front of the mirror. She forced herself to do an assessment of herself. Twenty-five, never been married. Not unattractive, but certainly not beautiful. She wasn't another Trixie, the blonde who looked gorgeous with damp lashes. Joy's hair was cut short and curly. With so many hours in the pool every day, it was the most practical style.

Turning sideways, she placed her hands on the underside of her breasts and lifted them. They were probably her best feature. If it weren't for those, most people would think she was a young boy. That was the problem with being so short. Petite, her mother claimed. Joy called it just plain stubby.

Within seconds Joy had determined she was headed for a lot of pain if she allowed this awareness for Sloan to continue. In all the years she'd been working, this was the first time she had faced these feelings. A patient was a patient, and she had never allowed herself to forget that. What had happened to destroy the protective veneer now?

The session with Sloan in the pool didn't go well. Both of them were on edge. The ability to work with one another, although grudgingly, was gone.

Sloan struggled to disguise his pain, and with every wince Joy had to force herself to continue. She didn't need to be reminded that it hurt. She knew.

"Are you going to do the exercises today or not?" Sloan questioned in a vicious tone, angry and impatient.

"Just what do you think I'm doing?" she shot back. Unconsciously Joy realized that she hadn't been working him as hard, because his pain was affecting her.

When the next series of manipulations had been completed, Sloan was left in little doubt that she was doing her job.

Later that afternoon, Joy entered the fenced yard to see L.J. The bird hobbled to her, and Joy bent down to talk to her creature friend.

"Hello."

L.J. squawked loudly, and Joy laughed.

"So you can talk. I was beginning to wonder." She held out her bandaged hand. "Did you see what you did?"

The gull tilted its head at an inquiring angle.

"Well, don't worry. I know it was an accident. But it was a good lesson for both of us." She crumbled up bits of fish and some other lettovers in his dish, then stepped back. Almost immediately L.J. began to eat. Joy stayed with him until he'd finished.

That evening she watched television with Paul, but a half-hour afterwards she couldn't have told anyone what she'd seen.

When she returned to her room, Joy couldn't decide if she should play her flute or not. But music was a basic part of her life, and she didn't know if she could go without it two nights running. Playing had always calmed her spirit and soothed her soul.

Her options were few. If she stayed in her room, she would be depriving Sloan of the pleasure he received when she played. It seemed almost petty to put her desire for solitude above what little enjoyment he received from life.

Dusk had cast a purple shadow across the horizon when Joy stepped onto the verandah. She paused to inhale the fresh scent of the sea and closed her eyes. The winds were whispering and gentle when she raised the musical instrument to her lips.

As always, the music flowed naturally from her. But tonight it was dark and deep, unlike the light tunes she normally enjoyed.

"You practicing for someone's funeral?" Sloan asked with a bitter tone.

Joy paused and lowered her flute. She'd been so caught up in the music she hadn't noticed he'd come outside. He stayed several feet away, his profile illuminated by the setting sun.

She shook her head. "No."

"Could have fooled me."

Ignoring him, she played again, forcing out a lively, popular tune. Before realizing what had happened, she slipped into the intense mournful music a second time. When she recognized what she'd done, she stopped midmeasure.

"Will you play at mine?" Sloan asked, his voice a mere whisper.

"Play at your what?" She didn't look at him, her gaze focusing on the tumbling waves that broke against the beach.

"My funeral."

"That's a morbid thought. You're not going to die," she said seriously, her own voice a soft murmur. "I won't let you."

His light laugh couldn't hide the pain.

"Do you want something?" She didn't need to explain what. When it came to painkilling drugs, Sloan was sensible. He never took anything unless the pain became unbearable. The fear of becoming addicted to the medication was always present, and he seemed well aware of the dangers.

He expelled a harsh breath before answering. "What I need is for you to kiss me better." His voice was low and seductive.

Joy didn't breathe; the oxygen was trapped in her lungs. Her hand tightly clenched the railing as she closed her eyes. The battle to alleviate the pain from his eyes with a gentle brush of her mouth over his was almost overpowering. The knowledge that one kiss would never be enough was the only thing that stopped her.

"Want me to call Trixie?" A fingernail broke against the freshly painted surface of the verandah. Still she didn't move.

"No." The word was released on an angry rush.

With her back to Sloan, she heard him return to his room.

Joy breathed again.

Stiffly Joy walked into the modern-style living room. "Good morning, Mr. Whittaker."

Myron Whittaker placed the coffee cup in the saucer and stood. "Morning."

"You asked to see me?"

"Yes, I did. Sit down, please." He motioned with his hand to the chair opposite him.

Joy sat on the edge of the velvet cushion and primly folded her hands in her lap. The Whittakers, although wonderful people, made her feel slightly gauche and ill at ease.

"How's Sloan?" his father began.

"There's been some improvement. I imagine within a few weeks he'll be able to start work on the mats and the parallel bars. From there it will only be a matter of time before he can advance to the walker and then the cane."

The older man lowered his gaze. "Yes, the cane."

Joy didn't need to be told what Sloan's father was thinking. "From what I can tell, your son will always have a limp. The cane will be necessary."

Myron Whittaker glanced up, and Joy had the funny sensation that although he was looking at her, he wasn't seeing her. "That's not it," he admitted absently, and shook his head. "I was remembering...thinking..." He let the rest of the sentence ebb away. "We used to play tennis, Sloan and me. Twice a week."

Joy could see no use in dwelling on things past. "It's unlikely that your son will play a decent game of tennis again."

He lifted the coffee cup to his mouth, and Joy noted that it shook slightly.

"I've done as you suggested and brought some work from the office. God knows I'm not able to keep up with it all."

"I think bringing Sloan back into the mainstream of his business can only help," Joy murmured, again feeling stiff and awkward.

"I was hoping to go over a few of the things with you."

"With me?" Her gaze shot to him. "Surely you don't expect me to discuss the business with your son?"

"To be honest, I was hoping you would bring up the subject with him. Sloan and I had a parting of ways on my last visit. At this point I feel it would be better if we didn't see one another for awhile."

"You can't mean that."

Myron Whittaker stood and paced across the thick white carpet. He propped his foot against the fireplace hearth, his back to her.

"Sloan and I have always been close. Don't misunderstand me, Miss Neilsen. I love my son."

"I'm sure you do."

"It hurts me to see him in that chair. There are so many things I wanted in life for Sloan, and now everything seems impossible." He dropped his foot and turned around. "The last time I saw Sloan we said some bitter, hard things to one another. I don't know if it would be a good idea for me to see him now. We both need time."

"But that's something you don't have," Joy countered, and released a slow breath. "Sloan regrets what happened just as much as you. Clear the air between you, make amends. Then bring up the business aspect of your visit. If you'd like, I could tell him you're here."

The agreeing nod wasn't eager. "If you think I should."

"I do."

Sloan was in his quarters, his head resting against the back of the chair, eyes closed.

When Joy tapped lightly on the open door, he straightened and opened his dark eyes, which narrowed on her.

"Your father's here to see you."

At first Sloan said nothing. "Tell him I'm busy."

"That would be a lie."

"When did you get so righteous?" Sloan tossed the question at her flippantly.

Joy made a show of glancing at her wrist-watch. "About five minutes ago."

Sloan ignored the humor. "I don't want to see him."

"He's your father," she shouted angrily.

"Do you want me to wave a banner?"

Maybe Joy wouldn't have reacted so strongly if her own father was alive. "That comment was unworthy of you, Sloan."

"Listen, Miss Miracle Worker. This is between my father and me. I'd advise you to keep out of it."

"No."

The barely controlled anger showed in the tight set of his mouth. His eyes were afire. "Stay out of this; it's none of your business. You seem to think you've got me wrapped around your finger. You're wrong. I refuse to allow you to dictate to me my personal affairs. Is that understood?" His voice gained volume with each word until the room seemed to shake with the sound. "Get out, Joy," he warned in a dangerous tone. "Get out, before I do something I'll regret."

She took a step in retreat, then stood her ground.

Sloan advanced his chair across the room until he was directly in front of her.

"He's your father," she murmured. "Don't do this to him. Don't do this to yourself."

"Stay out of it, Neilsen," Sloan ground out between clenched teeth.

In the past Joy had found ways around Sloan's pride. Now, facing his steel-hard resolve, she felt defenseless. There was nothing she could say or do.

Sloan's father stood when she entered the living room.

"I can tell by your face what he said. Don't bother to explain."

"I'm sorry, Mr. Whittaker," she added in a weak voice. "I feel terrible."

"Don't." He smoothed the hair along the side of his head and reached for his coat.

"I shouldn't have forced the issue."

He snapped the briefcase closed, his back to her. "Give me a call when you think..." Again he let the rest of the sentence trail away.

"I will." Joy walked with him to the front door. "I'm sure everything will work out fine."

Gravely he shook his head. Not for the first time, Joy noted the tired, hurt look in his eyes.

She stood on the front steps until his car rounded the bend in the road. Without questioning the wisdom of her actions, she marched through the house and into Sloan's room.

"That was a despicable thing to do."

"I told you to stay out of it," he stormed back.

"I won't."

Sloan escaped onto the verandah.

"You can't do this to your own father. He loves you. Seeing you like this is tearing him apart."

"You're right, it is," Sloan shouted, appearing in the doorway that led outside. "Don't you think I can see the pity in his eyes? He's no different from anyone else. I don't want his sympathy. I can't stand to see that look in his eyes."

Some of the intense anger drained out of her. "I'd give anything to have my father look any way at me," she whispered.

"Don't confuse the issue with sentimentality."

"Oh, Sloan," she moaned, and exhaled a wistful sigh. "Can't you see what you're doing? You're driving everyone who loves you out of your life."

"That's my choice," he returned bitterly. "I can see and do as I please."

"But you can't play tennis with your father."

The color fled from his face as his eyes hardened into cutting diamond chips. Fierce anger shot out from him. "You're right about that, Miss Miracle Worker. I'm not going to play tennis with my father. But then, I'll never play again, so what's the difference?"

The urge to fall to her knees and hold him was so strong that it was all Joy could do to turn and walk away.

To say Joy was miserable was a gross understatement. Paul attempted to lighten her mood by taking her out to dinner.

"I blew it." They sat at an umbrella table at Mobey Jake's. The neon whale flashed directly above them.

"Don't be so hard on yourself, kid."

Joy nearly choked on a french fry. "Kid?" she repeated. "How old do you think I am?"

The muscular shoulders lifted with a heavy shrug. "Twenty, maybe."

"Thanks." Joy laughed.

Paul laid his fish on a napkin and looked up thoughtfully. "You should laugh more often."

One corner of Joy's mouth lifted in a bittersweet smile. "There's not much excuse to laugh in this business. I wish my patients could understand that it hurts me as much as them."

"One patient, you mean," Paul inserted.

Joy looked out over the coastline instead of directly at Paul. "One patient," she agreed.

"Are you falling for this guy?" A frown marred his forehead.

Paul was nothing if not blunt. Joy felt the heavy thud of her heart. It beat so loud and strong that it seemed someone was pounding on her with a hammer. She reacted that way when someone spoke candidly.

"I hope not," she replied truthfully. "I've enough problems handling Sloan Whittaker without involving my emotions."

"If you need a shoulder to lean on, let me know."

"Thanks, Paul." Joy meant that sincerely. She'd never worked with nicer people than Paul and Clara.

It was dark by the time they returned to the house. Since Clara had the day off, Joy had cooked Sloan's dinner, and she was grateful when Paul had delivered it to him. When Clara returned, Paul and Joy had decided to eat out.

The porch light was on, but the house was dark. As Joy let herself into her room she noticed there were no lights on in Sloan's. Apparently he'd opted for an early night.

Not wishing to wake him, Joy carried her flute down to the beach. She stopped long enough to check L.J. and give him the left-over fish. The bird seemed to want out, and when Joy held open the gate, L.J. hobbled after her.

The two found a log not far from the house. Joy sat, buried her bare feet in the sand, and began to play. For a while L.J. stayed close to her side, but it didn't take much time for him to stray. As long as she could see him, Joy let him wander. The difficulty came when it was time to return to the house. L.J. enjoyed his taste of freedom and wasn't willing to go back to the small fenced area. Joy had to round him up like a sheep dog herding a stray lamb.

Laughing and breathless, she let herself into the house.

"What were you doing out there?"

Sloan.

"What are you doing up?" Joy had never known Sloan to come into the kitchen.

"I asked you first." The room remained dark.

Joy's eyes soon adjusted to the room's interior. Only a few feet separated her and Sloan.

"I . . . I was on the beach."

"That much I knew."

"Why are you here?" Her hand gripped the knob behind her.

"I heard you playing."

"I'm sorry if I woke you," she interrupted. "I didn't mean to."

Sloan wiped a hand over his brow. "I couldn't sleep. Did you and Paul have a good time?"

"Yes. We went to Mobey Jake's."

"Bring me anything this time?"

"No, I'm sorry. I didn't."

He dismissed her apology with a wan smile. "What took you so long coming inside? I was worried."

Sloan concerned about her? After this afternoon he had all the more reason to want her out of his life. In her eagerness to mend the rift between father and son, she had only done harm. Sloan was right; it wasn't any of her affair.

"Joy?" He seemed to be waiting for her answer.

"I was bringing L.J. home."

"You and that bird." His mirthless laugh was filled with irony. "I was ready to call out the National Guard."

"I really am sorry—for everything," she muttered.

Her apology produced a stunned silence.

"Did I hear you right? Joy Neilsen, gutsy Miracle Worker, actually admitting to a fault? Are you feeling well? Do you need a doctor?"

"I'm fine," she said with a shaky laugh. "Sloan, I feel terrible about today. You were right. I should never have stuck my nose where it doesn't belong."

The teasing laughter drained from his eyes. He extended a hand to her, palm open.

Scooting out a kitchen chair, Joy sat so that their gazes were level. With moisture seeping into her eyes, she placed her hand in his.

"Friends?" he questioned.

Joy nodded. "I prefer it to being enemies."

His hand closed tightly over hers, his thumb sensuously rotating against the inside of her wrist. "I do too." His eyes holding hers, he lifted her fingers to his mouth.

Joy tugged, and immediately Sloan released her hand. The potential for danger was powerful and strong. If she let Sloan kiss her fingers, it wouldn't be enough; she'd want to taste his mouth over hers and feel his hands on her breasts. She couldn't risk weeks of hard work for something as fleeting as physical attraction.

Awkwardly she stood and backed away. "Good night."

Somehow Joy managed to keep from running into her room. By the time she closed the bedroom door, she was trembling. Covering her face with both hands, she paced the blue carpet, her heart pounding like a trapped fledgling. Either she come to her senses or resign from this case. The matter was simple. She was a professional therapist, sensible and proficient. She knew better than to nurture this physical attraction. In the end she would leave the cripple, not Sloan. But just as she recognized she must rein in her feelings, she knew she couldn't bear to leave him now.

Joy was in the pool doing laps when Paul brought Sloan to the water's edge. Once placed on the side of the pool, Sloan could lower himself into the blue depths.

Treading water at the deep end, Joy waved. "I'll be right there."

"Don't hurry on my account," he shouted back.

A smile flashed from her eyes, and with powerful strokes Joy swam toward him.

"You look bright and cheerful this morning." Sloan had been up, dressed, and eating breakfast by the time Joy returned from her run. Unusual, since he normally delayed starting the day as long as possible. Joy could remember the first few days after her arrival and the struggle she had had just to keep his drapes open. Sometimes she forgot how far they'd come. But seeing him now, she was reminded how much farther they yet had to travel.

Clara hurried onto the patio. "Sorry to bother you, but Mr. Whittaker Senior is here."

A hardness stole over Sloan's face. "Who does he want to see this time?" The question was barely civil.

Joy bit into her lip to restrain an angry response.

Clara wiped her hands on her apron, obviously flustered. "Mr. Whittaker says he wants to talk to you." She directed her answer to Sloan.

"Tell him I'm busy."

"We can do this later," Joy inserted eagerly. "I'll come back..."

"No." His angry shout shut her off.

"Sloan, please," she whispered.

"Do as I say, Clara." He directed his attention to the housekeeper, his dismissal final.

With a quick bob of her head, Clara turned and hurried toward the house.

His narrowed gaze swung to Joy. "Was this brilliant idea yours?"

Joy returned his stare speechlessly. Was Sloan implying that she had sent for his father?

"Is it?" he shouted.

"Of course not. What are you suggesting?"

"I saw the two of you together," he hissed. "I'm not stupid. You two have something up your sleeves. Let it be known right now. I don't want any part of it. Is that understood?" The last words were shouted.

"Something up our sleeves?" Joy echoed incredulously. "Your father is half killing himself to maintain the business. *Your* company, I might add. He's dying in stages. In case you'd forgotten, your father's retired." Joy paused to draw in a breath. "Have you stopped to think what happened to him after your accident? Not only is he worried sick because of you, but he's taken over your position in the company—with all the stress and worries. But you, Mr. High and Mighty, you're so caught up in self-pity, all you see is yourself."

Sloan's face became sickeningly pale. "You don't know what you're talking about."

"Are you accusing me of lying now, too?"

"What can you expect me to think? They told me Harrison was in charge of the company."

"Have you looked at your father lately, Sloan, really looked? Can't you see what's happening to him?"

He was completely still, like a lion alert before the attack. "If what you say is true, it's Dad's own fault. He should have given everything over to Harrison the way he said he was."

"Are you really so uncaring?" His lack of concern shocked her.

His blistering hot gaze swept over her contemptuously. "What do you know of any of this?" he shouted. "Safe and warm in your secure little world, it must be easy to sit in judgment of something you'll never comprehend." A muscle worked convulsively along the line of his jaw.

The desire to tell him was overpowering. "What do I know?" She repeated his question with a half laugh. "Maybe it's time you found out exactly what I do." She swam to the steps that led out of the pool. "You asked me once about pain. Believe me when I tell you I'm well acquainted with it." She stood and placed one foot on the painted step. "You told me once you'd lain in a hospital bed wanting to die. I did more than want. I begged." Tears filled her eyes.

She turned to him then, the hideous scars that marked her thighs in full view. When she glanced at him she was prepared for the shocked look, even the repulsion he couldn't hide. She'd viewed it before when others saw her scars.

"Paul," she yelled, and hurriedly donned her terry cloth wrap. "Mr. Whittaker wants out of the water." Unable to bear another minute in Sloan's presence, Joy turned and ran into the house.

Five

"Joy," Sloan called after her, but Joy only increased her pace.

Paul met her halfway to the house. He stuck out a hand and stopped her. "You okay?" His finger brushed a tear from her cheek.

"Fine," she lied. "I'm fine."

Clara gave her a funny look as Joy came through the kitchen, but she didn't stop to explain.

Once in the privacy of her room, Joy slumped into a chair and covered her eyes with one hand. She'd only been sixteen at the time of the accident. A school cheerleader. But she would never be again. The scars were cleverly disguised with the proper clothing, so that no one need ever know. But their ugliness affected her more mentally than physically. She ran, she swam, she played tennis, could, in fact, do almost as much as before the accident. She had her father to thank for that, but even he couldn't force the look of shock and revulsion from people's eyes when they saw her misshapen thighs for the first time.

Joy changed back into her crisp nurse's uniform and held a cool washcloth over her eyes, hoping the cold water would take away the puffy redness. Tears were the last thing she wanted Sloan to see. He held enough aces in his hand as it was.

Clara was stirring something at the stove when Joy entered the kitchen. "Mr. Whittaker's been saying lots of things he don't mean lately," she commented, her back to Joy.

"Mr. Whittaker didn't say anything to upset me, so don't blame him for something he didn't do. He's confused enough without all of us turning on him." It would be unfair to have the others think Sloan had caused her to cry.

"I still think Mr. Whittaker had better take a long look at himself."

Joy pretended not to hear. "Do you mind if I take some of these leftovers to L.J.?"

"Isn't that bird well yet?"

"No. It'll be a long time before his wing heals completely."

"Go ahead, then."

"Thanks, Clara." She took out bits and pieces of meat and fish she knew the gull would eat.

Joy spent a good portion of a half-hour with L.J. He allowed her to touch him freely now— a small victory, but one that encouraged her.

When she came back into the kitchen, Sloan's lunch tray was ready.

"Take it in to him while it's hot."

Joy hesitated. She'd rather not see Sloan. He was sure to ask her questions she'd prefer not to answer.

"Go on," Clara ordered.

The door was open, and Sloan appeared to watch her anxiously. Joy was sure a niggling uncertainty showed in her eyes.

"Set the tray outside today," Sloan ordered. "I feel like looking at the ocean."

Still and silent, Joy did as he asked. He joined her at the round, enameled table on the verandah. He examined his lunch, lifting the warming dome and unrolling his silverware from the linen napkin. "Did Clara forget the pepper?"

Briefly Joy's eyes scanned the tray. She was sure she'd seen it earlier. "Would you like me to bring you some?"

"Please."

With obvious reluctance, Joy returned to the kitchen.

Sloan's eyes followed her as she came onto the deck. "Will you have your lunch with me?"

She focused her gaze on the view of the sky and the sea. A light breeze ruffled the silky, soft curls. Absently she smoothed the hair from her face.

"Joy?" he prompted.

She blinked, forcing herself to look at him. "Not today."

"Tonight then?"

Joy felt drained. "Why?"

"I think we should talk."

"About what?"

Sloan expelled an impatient sigh. "There's no need to be obtuse."

She whirled around to face him then, hands clenched so tight that her long nails cut into her palms. "Like everyone else who's seen my disfigurement, you're dying of curiosity. What happened? How long ago? Whose fault was it? I'm not a morbid sideshow."

"I wasn't thinking that at all," he said tautly.

"Don't lie to me. You're no different. Did you think you could hide the revulsion? Don't you realize I've seen abhorrence enough to recognize it?" she accused him in a choked voice.

"That's not true."

"Oh, for heaven's sake, spare me." Joy shook her head, not wanting to argue. Pointedly she placed the pepper shaker on the table and left.

As she walked away, Joy could almost feel the dagger penetrate her back. Sloan was angry. She had watched as he struggled to control his temper. For the first time in her memory, he'd succeeded.

Joy waited until Paul came for Sloan after lunch before she returned his tray to the kitchen. He'd hardly touched his lunch. But then, neither had she.

Adjusting a wide-brimmed straw hat on her head, she took a well constructed straw basket and headed for the beach. On several occasions she'd wanted to go beach-walking to look for seashells, but had yet to bring back more than one or two. The need to explore, to escape, to get away, was stronger today than ever.

When she stopped to check L.J. she noted he was quickly finding his protective home a prison and she decided to bring him with her. Readily the bird hobbled behind her when she opened the fence gate.

Her first find was an unbroken sand dollar, and she bent over to retrieve it from the wet shore. As she did, L.J. came to her side. He pecked away at grass, eating bugs and things she decided she'd prefer not to know. The two of them were content and happy. Two against the wind, two against the sea. Two cripples against the world.

The day was perfect as only a California springtime can be, and when Joy turned back to return to the house, she noticed the figure in a wheelchair coming toward her.

She paused, her feelings undecided. One half of her was demanding that she run the other way. Avoid him as much as possible, cast his curiosity and pity away. But the other half of her yearned for the comfort and understanding that could only come from another facing like circumstances.

There was irony here. None of her other patients had ever known. But she had never worked with anyone like Sloan Whittaker. His effect upon her was far more powerful than anyone else's, which made him dangerous in ways she still hadn't fully comprehended.

With L.J. hobbling behind her, Joy slowly sauntered toward Sloan.

"How'd you get out here?" she questioned when they met. Her eyes refused to meet his.

"You're a smart girl. Figure it out."

Hoping to display a lack of concern, she lightly shrugged her shoulders.

"Is it so dark and horrible that you can't tell me?" The question was issued so softly that for a moment Joy wasn't sure he'd spoken.

"It happened a long time ago. Some things are best forgotten."

"What you mean is the painful memories."

"I'm not going to argue, if that's what you want."

"It's not."

She stood stiffly at his side.

"Show me what you found?" he requested gently.

Joy didn't know how to deal with him when he was being kind and tender. She felt more comfortable dealing with his pride and anger.

When she didn't immediately respond, Sloan took the basket out of her hand and fingered the assortment of shells and rocks she'd collected. He lifted his eyes and his frowning gaze studied her. "You didn't want me to know, did you?"

"No," she quipped.

"You would never have told me if it hadn't been for my fight with my father."

Joy's eyes met his. Was that pain she heard in his voice? "Probably not."

"Why?"

"Why?" She angrily threw the word back at him. "You like perfection, especially in your women. I saw Trixie. The china-doll face, the figure a woman like me would die for. She's perfect right down to the mascara on the tips of her lashes and the uniformly shaped fingernails."

Her words seemed to anger him. "You're not like Trixie."

"That's just what I said," she shouted.

"Not in the ways that matter."

Her voice quivered as she struggled not to reveal the hurt his words inflicted. "I can't tell you how many times kindhearted people with good intentions told me that it didn't matter if I was scarred because it was what was on the inside that counted. I don't need to hear it from you."

"Now you're twisting my words."

She shook her head and pinched her lips together.

"You are the most incredibly beautiful woman I know."

Joy released a short, disgusted sound and stormed away. His rolling laughter stopped her. "What's so funny?" she demanded, swiveling around, hands on her hips, feet spread in a defensive stance.

"You are!" he shouted, the wind carrying his words. "Don't you remember how you said it was a sad commentary on my life if I needed you to rescue me from beautiful women?"

"I remember." She didn't lessen the distance separating them.

"I tell you how beautiful you are and immediately you act like I've given you the biggest insult of your life."

"I am not beautiful," she shouted back.

"Then why do I have to struggle not to kiss you? Why do I lay awake at night and wish you were in bed with me?" The violence in his voice stunned her.

Joy flinched at his words. "You don't know what you're saying."

"You're right. Not only am I a cripple, but I'm weak in the head."

"I won't argue with you about that." A gust of wind nearly lifted the hat from her head. Joy caught it just before it flew off. Long John squawked, diverting her attention, and when Joy looked at Sloan he had his back to her and was slowly progressing along the beach.

Unwilling to join him, but equally unwilling to leave him on his own, Joy sat and waited. She lay back in the sand and rested her eyes. Was Sloan attracted to her? The thought was heady enough to cause her heart to beat wildly. Sloan Whittaker was more tempting than any man she had ever known. But she would never fit into his world. Sloan was best left in the hands of women like Trixie. The two of them belonged together. She was only a therapist that would pass in and out of his life in short order. A year from now he'd have trouble remembering her name. Joy couldn't afford to lose sight of that.

She must have drifted into sleep. The next thing Joy knew Sloan let out an angry curse, and she sat up, surprised.

"You can call off your attack bird."

"Long John," she yelled. Sloan was sucking the side of his index finger.

"What happened?"

"Nothing."

"And you always suck your finger?"

"I do when it's bleeding."

"Let me see."

"No."

"My, my, aren't we brave," she murmured, coolly aloof.

"If you saw this cut you'd think so in earnest."

"Sloan, please. Did L.J. hurt you?"

"Only my pride. It seems your feathered creature doesn't make friends easily."

Joy gave a frustrated sound and fell to her knees at his side. "For heaven's sake, quit acting like a child and let me have a look at it."

His hand cupped the side of her face, raising her eyes to meet his. A heavy sensual awareness rippled through her, and it was all Joy could do not to place her hand over his and close her eyes. She was tampering with fire, and she knew it.

"It . . . it doesn't look bad."

"I told you it was only a scratch."

"I wouldn't want . . ."

"What wouldn't you want?" His voice was low and seductive as his hand cupped the other side of her face. "I can't help this," he whispered huskily. "Hate me later." His mouth gently kissed her chin, her eyes, the end of her nose, and caressed her cheek before softly parting her lips.

She should have stopped him. It wasn't him she'd hate later, but herself. Her arms slid around his neck; her fingers stroked the hair that grew thick there.

Sloan's mouth sought hers, and she moved her face against his until finally, when their lips met, Joy was beyond coherent thought.

The kiss was hard and demanding and showed an expertise she hadn't known from others. The tip of his tongue outlined her lips. Joy thought she would die from the pure pleasure as his mouth crashed down over hers.

His hand slid down her nape, his thumb moving in a slow rhythmic circle against her sensitized skin. He pushed the neckline of her dress off one smooth shoulder, his mouth blazing a trail of soft kisses that led to the scented hollow between her breasts. When Joy emitted a small protesting sound, Sloan tightened his hold and raised his mouth to the nape of her neck.

"Don't say it," he ground out in a fierce whisper. "I know what you're thinking."

"You couldn't possibly know."

"For once in your life, don't think. Feel." His mouth was on hers, hard with a hungry demand. The kisses became longer, more languorous, as he pressed their upper bodies as close together as possible.

"No...no..." She dragged her mouth from his. Stiffening, she pulled away. At first Sloan didn't want to let her go; Joy could sense as much as he tightened his grip. But after the first sign of struggle he released her.

Joy slumped on the sand beside him.

"Don't say it." The command was whispered harshly.

"I won't," she returned unsteadily. "I...I think we should get back to the house."

"Not yet." His voice was softer. "Sit with me for a while."

Joy's first reaction was to refuse. Together, alone like this, was dangerous for both of them.

She brought her knees up and circled them with her arms. For a long time they sat in silence. When she felt Sloan's gaze on her she turned to face him. Their eyes met. Hers soft, lambent, the effect of his kisses evident; his tired, strained.

Joy looked away. "I was only sixteen." Her voice was barely above a weak whisper. "I was a cheerleader on the way home from a Friday night game when the school bus was hit by a train. I...I don't remember much of the accident. Only the sound of screams and realizing they were my friends' and my own. My father told me I was trapped inside. Everyone told me how lucky I was to be alive." She gave a sad laugh. "For a long time I didn't think so. At least if I was dead the pain would go away."

"I thought the same thing," Sloan added in a gruff whisper. His hand rested on her shoulder as if some contact with her, even the light touch of his hand against her bare skin, was necessary.

"The doctors assured my family I'd never walk again. The damage was too extensive, multiple. My father wouldn't accept that. He insisted on a therapist." She paused and bit into her bottom lip. "It hurt so much I thought I'd die."

"And I once asked what you could possibly know about pain." His voice was filled with self-directed anger.

"You didn't know. My mother couldn't stand to see me suffer like that. I know it wasn't any easier on Dad, but he was there every session encouraging me, loving me, helping in any way he could. I'd be in a wheelchair today if it wasn't for my father."

"You told me once the only man you'd ever made cry was your father."

Joy nodded. "With the therapist's help, Dad learned the manipulations and assumed some of the exercises. I wanted to give up so many times. But Dad wouldn't let me. He prodded, pried, bribed, and when the pain was the worst he cried with me. But not once in the next two years would he let me quit."

"It took two years for you to walk again?"

"Two of the longest years of my life."

"I can imagine."

"If it weren't for the scars I don't think anyone would guess."

"No. Have you ever considered plastic surgery?"

Joy stiffened defensively. "My medical bills were staggering. My family gave me back my life. The disfigurement can be hidden. No, the thought has never entered my mind."

"I've offended you and I didn't mean to. I'd like to do that for you, Joy. My gift to you for everything you've done for me."

"I haven't done anything."

"How can you say that?"

"Easy. Want me to do it again?"

"Joy." He ground out her name in anger and frustration. "Why is it every time I try with you it backfires? I think you're wonderful just the way you are. The scars don't bother me. Keep them, if you like."

"I like." She stood and brushed the sand from her dress. "Paul and Clara will be worried. We should head back. Do you want me to push you?"

"No."

Joy had gone several feet, but Sloan didn't follow. When she glanced back expectantly, she saw that he hadn't moved, his gaze resting on the rough ocean. "You coming?" she called.

He turned toward her and nodded, but it was several long moments before he did so.

By midnight the house was as quiet as a funeral parlor. Joy remained in her room reading, or at least made the pretense of involving herself with a best-selling mystery plot.

The light tap against the sliding-glass door that led to the verandah startled her. She threw back the covers and quickly donned her housecoat.

"I couldn't sleep either." Sloan sat outside the door. "Don't lie and tell me you weren't awake."

"I was up," Joy conceded.

"Why didn't you play tonight?"

Since their meeting on the beach, Joy had avoided Sloan as much as possible without arousing suspicions. "I didn't feel up to it."

"Don't kid yourself. You weren't up to facing me."

"All right," she stormed. "I didn't want to see you. But it didn't do me much good, did it?"

"I can be as stubborn as you. Come out here and sit awhile."

Joy doubted that. "It's late." She searched for an excuse.

"That's never stopped you before. I bet you didn't know I could see you out here with your flimsy silk nightgown pressed against you in the wind."

Joy decided the best thing to do was refuse to be drawn into his game. "I'm hungry," she said on a falsely cheerful note. "I think I'll fix myself a sandwich. Do you want one?"

"You know what I want," he whispered as he carried her hand to his lips.

"No!" She pulled her fingers free as if his touch were red hot. She didn't know what he wanted. Didn't even want to guess, because whatever it was, her heart was willing. "I'm going to the kitchen."

"Then I'm coming too."

Her heart seemed to plunge into her stomach. Was there no escape? "It's your house," she returned with remarkable calm.

His laugh was short and mirthless. "At least we can agree on something."

Joy sliced a banana into thin pieces and laid them across a thick layer of peanut butter on bread. "Want half?"

Sloan's look was skeptical. "Peanut butter and banana?"

"It's good. Honest." She handed him half and poured them each a glass of milk.

Sloan joined her at the table. "I've been thinking all night of ways to thank you. But I never did have a way with words."

"Thank me?" She regarded him quizzically.

"I know what it cost for you to tell me about your accident. Even now, just talking about mine produces a cold sweat."

The bite of sandwich nearly stuck in her throat. She swallowed around it and reached for the milk. As she stood, the chair scraped against the floor. "I think I'll go see to L.J. before going back to my room."

"Running, Joy?" he taunted softly.

She was glad her back was to him so that he couldn't see the flame of color that flooded her face. "You're being ridiculous."

"I'll see you in the morning."

"Good night, Sloan."

The pause was only momentary before he whispered his own farewell. "Night, Joy."

Clara was busy in the kitchen when Joy returned from her run early the next morning. "Yum, that smells good. What is it?" Joy peeked under the lid of something cooking on the stove.

"Food. Now scat."

With a laugh, Joy took an apple off the table centerpiece and took a bite out of it. After a long run, she felt exhilarated.

"Here." Clara stopped her. "Take Mr. Whittaker his tray, will you?"

"Already?" Sloan wasn't normally up at this time.

"Yes, he was calling me soon after you left."

Clenching the apple with her teeth, Joy carried the tray down the long hallway. Her knock went unanswered. Resting the breakfast on one knee, she turned the knob and walked unheralded into Sloan's quarters.

Two steps into the room she stopped cold. Sloan and his father were busy going over some papers. Both father and son were so intent, neither was aware she was there.

Six

The apple fell out of her mouth, bounced, and rolled across the floor.

Myron Whittaker glanced up from the paperwork spread on the top of the large oak desk. "Good morning, Miss Nielsen. Could you set that tray outside? I'm hoping Clara sent an extra cup. I could use coffee this morning."

Sloan's expression was brooding. "Joy's my nurse, not a servant."

"I . . . I don't mind," she stuttered. "Really." She placed the breakfast tray on the verandah and come back through Sloan's room.

"Joy." Sloan stopped her. "Good morning."

His smile was devastating, her answering one weak but happy. "Good morning." A flowing warmth seeped into her limbs as she exited from the room.

"Does she normally dress like that?" Sloan's father's words followed her into the hallway. With a half-laugh, she bit into the corner of her bottom lip. She was wearing baggy gray sweatpants and an old T-shirt.

Mindful of her appearance, she returned with the extra coffee cup and picked up the apple that had rolled halfway under Sloan's bed. "I'll be out of your way in a minute."

"No problem," Sloan assured her. She left in a rush, but not before she caught the look of concern in Myron Whittaker's eye as he glanced from Joy to his son.

Joy didn't need to be told what he was thinking. Sloan's father was worried. He didn't want Sloan to fall in love with her—and with good reason. Joy wasn't stupid. Myron's picture of Sloan's future wife was someone like Trixie—as well it should be. Joy would never fit into the Whittakers' world; Sloan's wealth and lifestyle were as foreign to her as propositional calculus had been in her college days.

Later, the spray from the shower relaxed her muscles and soothed her body, but the look in Myron Whittaker's eyes continued to disturb her. He was right—she couldn't argue with him. Now she had to do her part to protect her heart and Sloan's.

Father and son worked until almost noon. Joy was sitting on a stool chatting with Clara when Myron walked into the kitchen. He looked relaxed, pleased, his eyes smiling.

"I owe you more than words can express," he said sincerely to Joy. "You've given me back my son. I'm going to see that you receive a generous bonus."

"Please, Mr. Whittaker, that's not necessary." The harsh lines of strain about his eyes and mouth had relaxed. That was all the appreciation Joy wanted to see.

"Nonsense." He dismissed her plea with a wave of his hand.

It was easy to see that arguing would do her no good. Myron Whittaker could be as stubborn as his son.

As soon as he left, Joy returned to Sloan's quarters to take back the breakfast tray and see if he was ready for their session in the pool.

"This was your idea, wasn't it?" he stormed as she walked into the room.

The anger in his voice stopped her. "Yes." She wouldn't deny it.

"Well, all I can say is thank God. You wouldn't believe some of the things that have been going on. How my father could make some of these decisions is beyond me."

A tiny smile broke out across her mouth. Joy battled to suppress it.

"What's so funny?" He didn't sound pleased.

"Nothing. Do you think you're going to have time to squeeze in the therapy today?"

Sloan set the papers he was working on aside. "I'll make the time."

Joy's mouth fell open.

"Don't look so shocked. You want to see me out of this thing, don't you?" He patted the rubber on the wheel of his chair.

"I'll get Paul and meet you in the pool."

"See you." He paused and glanced at his wrist-watch. "Fifteen minutes?" He made it a question.

"Fine."

Joy was doing laps when Paul delivered him to the pool. Sloan sat on the edge watching her.

"Don't you ever get tired?" he called after a while

Joy stopped and treaded water. "You should have said something. I didn't know you were there."

"You look like a sea nymph. That turquoise suit in the blue water leaves little to the imagination." His look was absent, his words thoughtful. "The scars were the reason you were always in the water ahead of me. It's also why you wear pants so much of the time."

Joy ignored his observations. She didn't want to talk about herself. "Are you going to come in or not?"

Sloan's smile was filled with warm amusement. "What will you give me if I do?"

"I think it's more of a question of what I'll do to you if you don't." The sound of his laughter rang in her ears as she swam toward him. She stood in the shallow end. "You're in a good mood today."

"Yes, I am," he agreed. "I can't tell you how good it feels to be needed again. Just looking over some of the things my father brought showed me how much things had slacked since I've been away." He lowered himself into the water. "You knew that, didn't you?"

"Everyone needs to know they're wanted."

"Even you?" The words were whispered on a husky breath.

"Even me," she returned crisply. "Now let's get to work."

"Always business. Don't you ever let loose and have some fun?"

"Of course I do. In fact, I'm going out tonight." The statement came off the top of her head. But the idea was a good one. She needed to check her apartment in Oxnard, a small town a few miles up the coast highway, and it wouldn't hurt to call a friend and make a night of it.

Sloan's mouth twisted, drawing in his facial features. The look in his eye chilled her. "Anyone I know?"

"I'm sure you don't. It isn't like we run in the same circle, is it?"

"No, I guess it isn't," he admitted, and stared at her.

Sloan was strangely quiet, almost brooding, for the remainder of their session. Even when she took him in his lunch, he did little more than give her a polite nod of acknowledgment.

That evening Joy's own feelings were mixed. She was sorry she'd said anything to Sloan about going out, and forced herself to dress in her best suit: lavender pleated pants and a pink silk blouse with matching lavender jacket. A strand of pearls graced her neck. While freshening her makeup, Joy tried to convince herself she was doing the right thing. The physical attraction between her and Sloan was growing more powerful every day. Of the two, she was the one who had to keep a level head, because she was the one who stood to lose the most. Her heart.

On the way out of the house, Joy stopped in the kitchen and told Clara where she could be reached in an emergency.

"I think it's time you took a day off, if you don't mind my saying so," Clara murmured as she dried the pots and pans from dinner.

"I don't mind," Joy agreed with a light laugh.

"Must say you look real pretty-like."

"Thanks, Clara."

"Don't suppose Mr. Whittaker's taken a look at you yet?"

"I haven't seen him since dinner." Quickly Joy changed the subject. "You know where you can reach me." Clara was much too observant not to have noticed what was happening between Joy and Sloan.

"Got it right here." She patted her apron pocket. "Let your hair down, girl."

"Honestly, it's only three inches as it is," Joy said with a small laugh as she opened the swinging door that led out of the kitchen.

She was in the marble-floored entryway when Sloan spoke.

"Don't you ever wear dresses?"

Joy stopped and turned. He was in the living room, almost as if he'd been sitting there waiting for her. His bitter, hard expression was a shock. Sloan hadn't looked like that since the first days after her arrival.

"Sometimes," she answered softly. "Usually full-length ones so I can be assured no one is going to be shocked if they happen to catch a glimpse of my scars."

"That's considerate of you," he muttered.

"It's not consideration. It's protection for my ego. These days women wear pants most anywhere, so it isn't any faux pas if I do."

His eyes held hers. "You look nice."

"Thank you."

"Have you decided where you're going yet?"

"Dan and I are going to dinner."

"Dan?"

"An old friend."

"How old?"

Joy inhaled a deep breath. "You're being ridiculous, you know that, don't you?"

"Like hell I am. Go on, go. Have a good time." Savagely he jerked the wheelchair around so his back was to her.

"Oh, boy, here it comes." Joy flew into the room and stood in front of him.

"Here what comes?" he barked.

"That 'poor little boy' act. You want me to feel guilty. You've even gone to great lengths so I'll experience this terrible guilt."

"Now you're the one being ridiculous," he declared, but his eyes refused to meet hers.

"Poor crippled Sloan has to sit home while nurse Joy paints the town." She raised her eyes heavenward in a mocking gesture. "I suppose you're planning to wait up for me, too?"

Sloan's nostrils flared as his eyes narrowed. "Get out of here."

"That's what I'm trying to do," she returned flippantly, and swung the strap of her purse over her shoulder in a defiant action.

She was halfway out the door when she heard him draw in a quick breath and utter something violent. Joy decided she would prefer not to know what he'd said.

The small apartment in the heart of town looked exactly as she'd left it. Joy walked around, inspecting each room. She'd only been back once since moving into Sloan's. The rooms were compact and unappealing after the luxury she was accustomed to living in these past weeks. In some ways Joy doubted that her simple life would ever be the same again. Certainly her heart wouldn't. If she had a whit of sense she'd pack her things and leave him now before their feelings for one another developed further.

A quick knock on the door was followed by a blonde head. "I thought I'd find you here."

"Hi, Danielle." The one thing about tonight that Joy regretted was letting Sloan assume she was seeing a man. It seemed childish now, but vital at the moment.

They ate at a Chinese restaurant and drank several cups of tea while chatting over old times. When Danielle suggested a movie, Joy readily agreed. After a quick phone call to Clara, she sat through a nondescript movie.

No matter how hard she forced herself to watch the screen, her thoughts continually drifted back to Sloan.

Danielle and Joy parted after the show, and Joy drove back to her apartment. Her watch said it was only ten. Much too early for her to head back to the beach house. If she was going to feel like a criminal because she took a night off, then he could sit and wait.

The television on, Joy slouched across a lumpy couch and laid her head against the back cushion and closed her eyes. When she opened them again it was well past two o'clock. Oh, heavens, she hadn't meant to stay that long. If Sloan had waited for her he'd be in a fine mood by now.

When she pulled into her parking spot in front of the house, she took in several calming breaths. Mentally she prepared herself—for what she wasn't sure.

The porch light was on, and another in the long hallway that led to her room. She turned off the outside light and tiptoed into the entryway. "You look like a thief in the night." A deep voice flew out from the living room.

Startled, she let out a gasp. Her hand flew to her breast. "What are you doing there?" she demanded defensively.

"In case you've forgotten, I live here."

"I didn't mean that to sound the way it did," she apologized. "You frightened me."

He moved closer to her. "Did you have a good time?"

"Wonderful," she lied.

"How was Dan?"

"Good." She took in a deep breath. "Is this an interrogation?"

"No, just curious interest."

"I didn't mean to stay out so late." She could have kicked herself the minute the words slipped past her mouth.

"Time flies when you're having fun, or so they say."

"Yes, well, I think I'll get to bed."

"Did Dan kiss you good night?" The question came abruptly, issued with impatience.

"I don't think that's any of your business." Her hand tightened around the strap of her purse.

"You don't look like you've been kissed."

"Sloan, please." She released the words on a whispering sigh.

"At least when I kiss you, there's no doubt. Your eyes grow warm and gentle, your face is flushed, and you have a look about you that begs for more."

Joy looked away, but not before she saw the way Sloan's fingers bit into the arm of his chair.

"Does Dan make you feel the way I do?" he continued, his voice raspy and deep. "Does your heart beat faster when he holds you? Or is it just the thrill of having a man, a real man, one you don't have to look down to?"

"Stop it," she cried, her voice strained and weak. "You don't know what you're saying." The temptation was to cry out that he was more man than she'd ever known, all the man she'd ever need. Were he never to take another step, she couldn't love him any more than she already did.

Joy inhaled a sharp breath, her eyes rounded at the startling realization. For days she'd been struggling with herself, refusing to accept the truth. Now, in her anger, she acknowledged her true feelings. It was too late; she was already in love with him.

"Joy?" Sloan paused and took her hand. "Are you all right? You look like you're sick."

"I'm fine," she mumbled, and pulled her hand free from his. "I just need to lie down." She felt like she was staggering as she rushed down the hall to her room. Of course, she wasn't, but it seemed her whole world had crumpled in on top of her and the weight was more than she could possibly manage.

"Joy, wait," Sloan called out after her, but she ignored him and firmly shut the bedroom door.

Even after she'd changed clothes and crawled between the fresh sheets, Joy couldn't sleep. Unreasonably, she was angry with Sloan. Irritated, because he knew as well as she what was happening between them and had done nothing to stop it. Her feelings, emotions, and heart were only playthings to him, a small diversion until he was walking again. She could almost hate him. Almost.

She lay there for what seemed like hours, unable to sleep because every time she closed her eyes pictures of Sloan would flash into her mind. Not content with dominating every waking minute, he was determined to haunt her sleep as well. The room felt hot and stuffy. Throwing back the covers, Joy opened the sliding-glass door just a crack. A faint moaning sound stopped her. She had to strain to hear. Sloan.

Was he in pain? Thoughtless of her bare feet, she slipped outside. Sloan's glass door was also cracked. The sound of his moans was more distinguishable now, in addition to a faint thrashing noise. Joy peeked inside his room.

Sloan was asleep and in the throes of some horrible dream. His head tossed from side to side, his blankets a twisted mess around his legs.

"Sloan." She hurried to his bedside and placed a restraining hand on both shoulders. "Wake up. You're having a dream." Lightly she shook him. "Sloan, it's a dream."

He jerked himself upright, leaning the brunt of his weight on one elbow. For a second he looked at her blankly, then released a small cry of relief. "Joy, good heavens." His eyes were filled with some unspeakable torment. Forcefully he pulled her into his arms, his breathing hoarse and uneven. "Oh, Joy." His open hands caressed her back, shooting a tingling fire down her spine. "I thought I'd lost you," he continued. "You were in the school bus screaming for me to help you, and I couldn't get out of the chair.''

''I'm fine, I'm right here,'' she assured him, her hands brushing the hair from his face. Her heart cried out to him.

''I couldn't bear to lose you now.'' He twisted his upper body, bring her onto the bed beside him. Positioned so that he was above her now, his anguished eyes stared into hers. ''Don't stop me. I need you so much,'' he murmured before his mouth rocked over hers.

She gave in to him unselfishly, parting her lips with all the eagerness of her newly discovered love. Her hands roved his back, reveling in the muscular feel of skin under her fingers. He was warm, vital, and for this moment, this night, hers.

His mouth left hers and pressed against the gentle slope of her bare shoulder.

''You've been drinking,'' she whispered.

''Yes.'' He continued to kiss her neck, his tongue making moist forays against the sensitive skin. ''It was the only thing that kept me sane tonight while waiting for you.''

''Oh, Sloan. You didn't drink after taking any medication, did you?''

"Don't 'Oh, Sloan' me. I know what I'm doing. For once stop being my nurse and be my lover?" His mouth blotted any objection she might have voiced.

Joy was reeling with the potency of his kisses. When his exploring hands cupped the soft undersides of her breasts, she released a small cry of pleasure. Gently his thumbs made lazy circles around her nipples until they turned to hard pebbles. She felt as if her breasts swelled under the gentle manipulations.

"You shouldn't," she protested weakly.

"Do you want me to stop?" he whispered against her ear, his warm breath caressing her lobe.

"No," she admitted, her arms entwined around his neck, "don't stop."

Desire, raw and fierce, ran through her blood, spreading a path of fiery awareness that left no part of her untouched. Her senses were in turmoil. No longer did she question right from wrong. No longer did it matter.

Sloan's kisses grew more deep, more passionate; their effect drugged her into submission and demanded a response. Trapped in the warm, rushing tide of her love, Joy responded freely, wholly. If Sloan had asked for her soul she would have handed it to him without thought—so deep was her love.

Deftly his hands pulled the silken material of her nightgown over her head and tossed it aside. Joy all but cried with the pleasure of his bare skin over hers. She moaned softly as his warmth seemed to brand her.

His lips began a downward path from the sensitive cord of her neck to her breasts and stomach. Her long fingernails dug into the rippling muscles of his back as she arched, wanting to give more, needing to receive more.

"Joy," he moaned, and bruised her mouth with a scorching possession. "Do you realize how long it's been since I touched a woman like this?"

The whole world came to a sudden, abrupt halt. A woman. Any woman would have done. She was convenient, here, now. A passing fancy until he was ready for the Trixies of this world.

Dragging her mouth from his, she violently pushed him away. "Don't," she cried, and struggled to sit up.

Sloan went still. "What is it? Have I hurt you?"

The question was almost ludicrous. She was dying, and he wanted to know if he had caused her pain.

"Joy?" He raised himself up and brushed the hair from the side of her face. "What's wrong?" His tender concern was nearly her undoing.

"Let me go," she cried, her voice pitifully weak. She shut her eyes, but a tear squeezed its way to her mouth.

"Not until you tell me what's wrong." His voice was thick with frustration. "You're crying?" A finger brushed the wetness across her cheek. "Joy, please. Tell me what I did."

"It has been a long time since you've touched a woman," she whispered achingly at last. "So long that you'd hold any willing woman."

"That's not true. I can't think of anyone else when you're in my arms. It's you I want," he muttered thickly. "Only you."

"That will change," she said confidently, "and soon."

He groaned her name.

"Please let me go," she pleaded, her voice quivering uncontrollably.

With a frustrated exclamation, Sloan rolled off her and stared at the ceiling as she searched for her nightgown. She paused long enough to slip it over her head and run as if the devil himself were in pursuit.

For two weeks they treated one another like polite strangers. To avoid the curious stares of Clara and Paul, Joy took long daily walks along the beach. No longer did she play her flute on the verandah at night. L.J. was her companion and friend, often trailing behind her on a walk.

On the first night of the third week, Joy delivered Sloan's dinner tray. He sat, his gaze centered on the ocean. Joy left it on the table outside.

"Can we talk?" he asked without looking at her.

Joy bit into the soft fleshy part of her inner cheek. "What do you want to talk about?"

"Us."

"No," she answered emphatically.

"All right, we won't talk about us. We'll simply talk."

Joy walked to the railing, watching the rumbling sea. The scent of the ocean filled the early evening. A gentle breeze brought in a

salty spray. She turned and propped her elbow
against the railing. ''I don't know if we have
anything to say to one another.''

''That's a negative thought. I've never
known you to be pessimistic.''

''Oh, I can be,'' she admitted with a sad
smile.

''Yes, I noticed.''

''If you don't eat, your dinner will get
cold.'' Her mouth felt suddenly dry, yet her
hands were moist to the point of being
clammy. She should have packed her bags and
walked out the next morning. But she couldn't,
not before it was time. When he was walking,
at least on crutches, then she'd go.

His gaze fell on the tray she'd brought with
her. ''Let it. I'm not hungry.''

''Have you been busy?'' she knew he met
daily with his father now, and she had seen his
light long into the night.

''Very.''

''That's good.''

He came closer to her side. ''In some ways
it's helped me . . .'' He let the rest trail away.

''Helped you how?''

His smile was wry. ''You said the subject
was taboo.''

"Oh," she said, and swallowed tightly.

Paul shouted from the far side of the yard and waved. Joy gave a guilty start. She'd told him she would join him for dinner at Mobey Jake's. They went there often now.

"I've got to go."

Sloan's mouth thinned with impatience. "I understand."

Quickly she moved into her own quarters and grabbed a light sweater.

"Joy." Sloan had followed her and slid open her glass door. "Will you play tonight? I've missed that." His smile was slightly off-center, and her bones felt like liquid. "Almost as much as I've missed having you as my friend."

"I've missed it too," she murmured, refusing to look into his eyes.

"Hurry back, my Joy."

The words were issued so softly Joy was sure she'd misunderstood him.

Paul brought her a double order of fish-and-chips and joined her at the umbrella-covered table in the sun. The large order was far bigger than Joy could manage, but she automatically bought the double fish so there would be enough for L.J.

"You and the boss getting on better?" Paul questioned. Their camaraderie and mutual respect had grown over the weeks. They were a team, pressing toward one goal—Sloan. He would walk one day, and the credit would be due them all.

"I guess so." She wiped the corner of her mouth with the napkin and lifted one shoulder in a lopsided shrug.

"Sometimes I wonder how you two can work with one another, the ice is so thick."

"You have a good imagination," Joy denied uneasily.

Paul lifted one thick brow expressively. "If you say so."

Joy dunked a french fry in a small container of ketchup. "I do."

Later, she brought her flute onto the verandah. She hadn't played three notes when Sloan joined her. She lowered her instrument and offered him a smile.

"Are you taking requests?"

"Sure, what would you like to hear?"

"Yesterday," he replied without hesitation.

Joy remembered the first time she'd played the song. Sloan had angrily proclaimed that yesterdays were gone forever, that they couldn't be brought back. Bitterness had coated his words. Now his voice was filled with hope.

The sweet melodic sounds of the Beatles' classic filled the night. Joy had always loved this tune. When she was finished, there was a poignant pause.

"Why did you request that song?" she asked in a whisper, not wanting conversation to ruin the mood.

"Because I wanted to share with you some of my yesterdays."

"How do you mean?"

"Follow me," he answered cryptically, and turned sharply, leading the way through his quarters. Once he was in the hallway he paused in front of the door that was opposite her room. "Haven't you ever wondered what was in here?"

"No," she answered honestly. "I assumed it was probably your parents' room."

"Go on, open it."

Joy turned the knob and stepped inside. Because his chair wouldn't fit through the narrow doorway, Sloan remained in the hall.

The interior was dark, and she felt against the side of the wall for the light switch. Once she located it, she flipped it on. Immediately light sprayed across a room filled with awards, trophies, and sports equipment. Plaques lined one entire wall. On closer inspection, Joy saw that each one had been received by Sloan. There didn't seem to be anything he hadn't tried and mastered. Baseball, volleyball, skiing, bowling, hockey, and some she had never known existed and probably couldn't pronounce.

Confused, she turned around, her smooth brow marred in thick creases. "All these are yours?" she asked incredibly. "It's unbelievable."

"I was quite the jock."

She picked up and inspected one of the smaller baseball trophies. "You were just a boy." She lifted her gaze to his.

"My father is credited with mounting most of these things. The albums on the desk—" he pointed to a large flat-topped desk on the far side of the room "—are filled with newspaper clippings from the time I could hold a tennis racket."

"My goodness, it's enough to take my breath away."

"I was good."

"I don't doubt it."

"I'll never be as good again."

Joy didn't mince words. "No, you won't. Does that bother you terribly?"

The look in his eyes seemed to peel away every defense barrier she'd carefully constructed these past two weeks.

"It did, but you changed that."

"Me?" The one word echoed across the room.

"I accepted the wheelchair as my fate—until you came. It wasn't a conscious decision, but one I can see as clearly now as if I'd signed the contract in blood. I was a winner with remarkable talent and skill, if I was to believe everything that had been written about me. I had the world by the tail; I lived the good life. And then it all came tumbling down on top of me. After the accident I decided that if I had to be half a man the rest of my life, then I'd be no man at all."

Joy understood what he was saying. She came and knelt by his side.

"It wasn't the pain that bound me to the chair, but the fear." He took her hand and squeezed it tight. "I'm going to walk again, Joy Nielsen, because you had the foresight to understand what was happening to me on the inside. And just as you had your father, I have you." Very gently he lifted her hand to his mouth and kissed it.

Her heart plummeted to her stomach. Gratitude was what Sloan felt. Overwhelming gratitude, nothing more.

Seven

"You're sure about this?" Sloan regarded her skeptically.

Joy sat on the thick blue mat on the weight-room floor, her legs crossed Indian fashion. "Trust me."

"You said that when you asked me to roll around like a man whose clothes had caught on fire."

"Now I want you to crawl just like a baby."

"How much longer before I can work on the parallel bars?" He eyed the set she'd brought in.

"Not long, I promise. If you want, I'll test you for strength again today."

"No." He shook his head, and Joy could all but taste his disappointment.

"Don't push yourself so hard. You're doing remarkably well."

"But the progress is so slow."

"It isn't," she replied emphatically. "Look how long you sat in that chair—months. You can't expect to be out running again in a matter of days."

"Tell me what's next."

Joy must have repeated the procedure to him fifteen times, but she didn't hesitate when he asked again.

"Lying to crawling, crawling to kneeling, kneeling to standing."

"From there to the parallel bars, the walker, and lastly the cane," he finished for her.

"There's a light at the end of the tunnel."

"I'm just beginning to see it."

"Good." She smiled brightly. "I knew you would."

"Should I pretend I'm a dog and bark?" he asked as he moved into the crawling position.

"Go ahead." Joy laughed. "It'll give Clara a good laugh."

Sloan gave an Academy Award performance that left both Joy and Paul laughing.

"Mr. Jewett's here. Ain't seen Dale in near nine months."

The laughter drained out of Sloan's face and his eyes turned icy cold. "Send him away. I don't want to see him. Is that understood, Clara?''

"But Mr. Jewett's been your friend since you was a boy."

"It doesn't matter. I don't want to see anyone."

Joy tossed a glance to the obviously flustered Clara, then back to Sloan. Angrily Sloan reached out from his position on the mat and grabbed the side of his wheelchair. With a violent shove he sent it crashing against the wall. The chair tilted onto its side and fell over.

"What's wrong?" she asked quietly, and knelt at his side. "Who is the guy?"

"A friend."

"You have a funny way of showing it."

"When I want your advice, I'll ask for it," he growled.

"That wasn't advice," Joy returned defensively. "I was simply stating an opinion."

"Then keep those to yourself."

"Fine." She stood and wiped the grit from her hands. Walking across the room, she uprighted the wheelchair and brought it to his side. "I want you to make the transfer yourself today."

"I can't."

"Don't give me that, Whittaker."

"What is this? Put the cripple in his place time?"

"Figuratively speaking, I think that's it."

"Get out of here, Joy, before I say something I'll regret later."

Joy's mouth formed into a humorless smile. "Gladly." Arms flying at her side, she stormed into the kitchen, plopped down on a chair, crossed her legs, and took three deep breaths.

"What's with that man lately? Mr. Jewett and Mr. Whittaker been good friends a lot of years. Friends shouldn't treat one another like that. It's not right, it's just not right. But no one pays a mind to ol' Clara. No one," she emphasized.

"What's the matter with me lately?" Joy answered Clara with a question of her own. "I used to give as good as I took."

Clara apparently chose to ignore Joy. "I said to Mr. Jewett that Mr. Whittaker not feeling himself today. That's what I said because I know later Mr. Whittaker is going to want to see his friends again. No need to offend them. I did right, didn't I?" Clara's look was eager.

"You did fine."

Clara clucked, and a look of relief relaxed the wrinkled face.

"Are you sure there isn't any reason Sloan wouldn't want to see his friend?"

"Mr. Whittaker sent all his friends away after the accident. He didn't want to see no one. Mr. Jewett came around for a long time, but Mr. Whittaker wouldn't see him. Same as now. It's not right to treat friends like that."

"What's not right?" Sloan entered the kitchen and boldly glared at the cook.

"To send friends away," Joy answered for Clara.

Briefly, renewed anger flashed from his eyes. "You two are beginning to sound like hen-pecking wives."

"Mr. Jewett's been your friend for a long time..."

With a burst of energy, Sloan wheeled himself out of the room, apparently not wishing to become involved in a heated argument.

Joy didn't see him again that afternoon. After his time with Paul, he met with his father and spent the remainder of the day in his room going over the papers his father brought.

Joy sat on the beach with L. J. until dinner, wondering if she should press this thing with

Sloan. She understood what he was doing all
too well. She'd done it herself. Friends, especially ones who were whole and well, were a
reminder of things that would never be again.
Even Danielle, her best school friend, the one
person who knew her so well, couldn't help or
understand the adjustment Joy was making. In
some ways Danielle hurt more than she helped.
She came to visit, eager to share tidbits of news
and gossip from school. Joy hadn't wanted to
know or hear any of it. School, boys, teachers
were so far removed from her life then that it
only served to widen the gap between them.

Sloan met Joy that night on the verandah.
She was sitting watching the sunset, a fiery ball
of orange lowering into the ocean.

Sloan pulled up beside her. "Beautiful, isn't
it?"

Smiling, Joy nodded. "I don't think I'll ever
get tired of looking at it. The whole world
seems so peaceful and serene. It's hard to remember the tragedies reported on the evening
news when everything's so calm here."

"I often feel that too."

She felt at ease with Sloan, relaxed, so unlike their first days of constant confrontation.
Those times seemed a million miles away now.

She turned to smile at him and noted the signs of stress about his mouth. His dark eyes looked tired.

"You're strung out from working all day," she whispered. "You should go to bed."

Teasing warmth kindled in his gaze as he smiled slightly. "Now that, my dear Joy, sounded suspiciously like an invitation."

The gibe was a gentle one, and Joy couldn't take offense. "No. When I issue an invite there won't be need for any speculation." Joy had hoped to sound breezy and sophisticated, but it came out all wrong. She could feel Sloan's puzzled gaze run over her.

"You're blushing, which leads me to believe you're still a virgin." His short laugh was soft, almost caressing.

Joy straightened. "I don't like the sudden turn of this conversation," she said stiffly. "Let's go back to what a beautiful sunset it is."

"Your cheeks are nearly as bright as the sky."

"Would you stop?" she demanded.

"No," he chided, and linked his hands behind his head, obviously enjoying himself. "Why?"

"Why what?"

"Why haven't you gone to bed with a man?"

"Honestly, Sloan, you're embarrassing me. Don't, please." She hung her head and pretended to be studying her fingernails. The sound of his moving drew her gaze. Sloan had turned his chair around and parked himself beside her so that only a few inches separated them. A finger under her chin turned her face to him.

"For most of my life I've stayed away from girls who didn't know the score. I wanted a woman with experience."

Joy swallowed uncomfortably. His eyes were tender, infinitely gentle.

"That was until I met you," he went on. "I'm pleased you are who and what you are. I wouldn't change a single thing about you for anything." His hand slid behind her neck, urging her mouth to his.

Confused and unsure, Joy stiffened; she knew what would happen if she let him kiss her. It would be lighting a match to gasoline. The feelings Sloan produced in her weren't a small spark, but a forest fire. She wanted him so much, but at the same time was all too aware of where it would lead.

He dropped his hand at her resistance. The puzzled look in his eyes deepened into pain. "Is it always no to every man?"

She looked away and nodded, because speaking was almost impossible.

"Is it the scars?"

"No."

"Then why?"

One shoulder was lifted in a halfhearted shrug, urgently hoping he'd change the conversation. "I'm not exactly a sex goddess."

"There's never been anyone I've wanted more."

Bounding to her feet, Joy stalked to the far side of the deck. "Stop. Please. I find this whole conversation extremely embarrassing."

"If I promise not to mention it again, will you come back and sit with me?"

Joy didn't find the teasing light in his eyes encouraging. "Promise?"

"Scout's honor." Solemnly he raised his index and middle fingers.

Joy returned to the cushioned wrought-iron chair and relaxed.

"But then, I was never a Boy Scout," he inserted.

"Sloan!"

"I promise, I promise."

Joy sat and brought up her knees, resting her chin on top of one. "Tell me about Jewett." Joy could sense him drawing away from her. Not physically, but mentally.

"He's a buddy," Sloan returned in a tone that discouraged further discussion.

"A good friend?"

Irritably, he expelled his breath before answering. "At one time."

"Not now?"

"I know what you're doing, Joy," he breathed impatiently. "And I don't like it."

A gentle breeze ruffled the soft curls about her face, and Joy laughed lightly. "I love turning the tables on you."

"I don't want to talk about Dale or any of the others."

"Why not?"

"Because—" he hesitated "—because I'm not the same person I was before the accident."

"Dale knows that. He doesn't need a psychology degree to realize you've changed," she explained in a patient voice.

"The only friend I need is you."

"But I couldn't possibly hope to meet all your needs."

He cocked his head, and a teasing smile flirted at the side of his mouth. "You could try."

Joy ignored the glint in his eyes. "I did the same thing to my friends. Looking back, it's easy to see that my ego was involved, because I didn't want anyone to see me like that. Nor did I want to hear who was going with who and what couple had broken up. My life had gone beyond all that, and it seemed trivial and petty. They'd come with pitiful looks and talk as if I'd had brain damage."

"Exactly," Sloan agreed.

"But I didn't consider the fact that they needed me. I was their friend, and they loved me. It hurt them to see me the way I was, and desperately my friends wanted to do something, anything to help. For a long time I wouldn't let anyone near me. Then one day Dani—"

"Dani?" Sloan questioned.

"Danielle, for real," Joy supplied.

"Not the old friend Dan you had dinner with not so long ago?"

"One and the same," she supplied with a puzzled look.

Sloan went completely still, and she watched as the muscles worked along the side of his jaw. "You little devil. You did that on purpose."

Too late, Joy realized exactly what she had revealed.

"Purposely you let me assume that you were going out with a man."

"Yes . . . well," Joy floundered.

"I sat here half the night going crazy thinking about you in the arms of this Dan. You should suffer for what you put me through." He wheeled around so suddenly, Joy was caught completely off-guard.

Somehow she managed to escape his grip as she scurried out of the chair. Laughing, she ran down the deck, Sloan in hot pursuit. When she'd gone as far as possible, she turned, the wood railing pressing against her back. Joy stretched out a pleading hand. "Sloan." She couldn't keep the laughter out of her voice.

"Yes, my trapped little rat?"

"Would it do any good to apologize?"

"Not when I've got you where I want you."
Slowly he advanced toward her, one inch at a
time.

"Sloan," she pleaded a second time. Frantically she looked around for an escape.

"Mr. Whittaker, where are you?" Clara's
high-pitched voice could be heard coming
down the hall. There was a slight hesitation as
the older woman stepped onto the verandah.
"Oh, Mr. Whittaker, I was hoping I'd find you
here."

"Yes, Clara, what is it?" Sloan's voice was
thick with impatience.

"If you'll excuse me." Joy sauntered out of
her corner and wickedly fluttered her long
lashes. "It seems to have gotten a bit chilly out
here all of a sudden. I think I'll take a drive
into town."

"Are you going to meet Dan again?" Sloan
taunted.

"Not tonight," she said with an exaggerated sigh. "But I think I'll give Mark a call."

His eyes narrowed for an instant before a
smile broke out across his powerful face. For
now she would escape, his eyes were telling her,

but the time was fast approaching when he would extract his due.

"Are you ready?" Joy's voice was soft with encouragement.

Sloan shook his head. Joy didn't know how he could be so calm. Her stomach felt like it had twisted to double knots. Even her mouth felt dry, her throat scratchy.

The parallel bars loomed before him. Sloan positioned the wheelchair so that he could reach up and pull himself upright.

Joy watched him with a ballooning sense of pride. Once he was upright, he beamed her an off-center smile.

"Well?" he probed. "How am I doing?"

Joy shook her head, because she was afraid the lump that filled her throat would make her words sound irregular and he would know how happy this new triumph made her. This was only the beginning.

"I don't think I realized how tall you are," she said at last.

Sloan continued to work his way across the bar, each movement cautious and measured. His face was furrowed with intense concentration.

"And I don't think I've ever realized what an elf you are."

"I am not," she denied hotly.

His laugh was rich and deep. He stopped when he came to the end of the long bars and awkwardly turned around.

Joy watched him with her heart in her throat. She need not have worried; he was doing wonderfully well.

"Joy," he called to her, and she was immediately at his side.

"Yes?"

"Stand here." He indicated a place beside the bars. When she did as he asked, he manipulated himself around so that they stood facing one another. She came to just an inch or two under his chin. "An elf," he affirmed, "but a perfect one. Look how well we fit together." A hand grazed her cheek and cupped her neck. "I've been waiting weeks to kiss you like this. Don't deny me now."

Joy could refuse him nothing. Had he asked for any part of her she would have given it to him gladly with all the love pent up inside.

When his lips touched hers, she released a small, weak cry of happiness. The kiss was sweet and gentle and left her craving for more.

Somehow Sloan managed to keep his balance as he cradled her head against his chest and pressed his face into her hair.

"Thank you, Joy," he murmured, and again she was reminded that his emotions were confused, interwoven with a deep sense of gratitude.

"Has something happened to Sloan?" Margaret Whittaker rushed into the living room. Her face was pale and tight. Myron Whittaker followed close on his wife's heels.

"Not at all," Joy hurried to assure them. This whole production was Sloan's idea, and she was reluctantly playing her role. "Please sit down."

Myron eyed his wife and shrugged his shoulders. "You say Sloan's fine?"

"Yes." For a moment she was sure her smile gave her away. "Perhaps you'd like some coffee while you're waiting?"

"Please," Myron answered for them both, and stopped to run a hand across his forehead.

Joy excused herself and rounded the corner, pretending she was going into the kitchen.

"You should be shot for this," she told Sloan in a heated whisper. "They're both worried sick."

He was standing. The U-shaped walker accepted his weight as his hands gripped the metal bar. Joy continued to marvel at how tall he was. Tall and vital. But even the wheelchair had been unable to diminish the aura of powerful virility that was so much a part of him.

A happy smile skittered across his face.

"What's so funny?" she demanded.

"You. I still can't believe I let such a pipsqueak boss me around. I must have been weak in the head."

"Not weak," she countered brightly, "but exceptionally smart."

He bent his head and kissed her lightly on the cheek. "Don't tell me to break a leg."

She smiled, one that came deep from within her heart. "All right, I won't."

With a slow gait, every step deliberate and practiced, Sloan moved out of his hiding position in the hall. Joy stayed where she was, the sound of his steps, the drag of the walker against the floor, magnified in the enclosed area. She didn't need to be told the cries from Sloan's parents were ones of surprise and happiness. In her own way she was inexorably happy. Yet the time was fast approaching when she must leave. Sloan wouldn't need her anymore.

"Clara, Clara." Myron Whittaker's voice boomed through the house.

Joy stepped aside as Clara bustled out of the kitchen.

"Bring out my best bottle of champagne. There's cause to celebrate again."

"Joy," Sloan called to her.

Purposely she had stayed out of view. This was a time for family; she didn't want to intrude.

"Joy," he repeated, and she stepped around the entrance to the hallway and into the living room.

"Where did you go?" he questioned, his eyes watching her, his look vaguely troubled. "I thought you were right behind me."

Margaret was dabbing the corner of her eye with a scented handkerchief, and when she saw Joy she hurried across the room and hugged her tightly. "My dear Miss Nielsen, Myron and I owe you so much."

"Dad's bringing out the family's best." Sloan's eyes were bright with excitement.

"Do stay, dear," Margaret insisted. "After all, it's you we all must thank."

"Nonsense." Embarrassment heightened the natural color in her cheeks.

Sloan wrapped an arm around Joy's thin shoulders. "Mother, we owe this little pint-sized woman more than words can express."

A look of undisguised concern flickered briefly over Margaret Whittaker's eyes. Joy saw it but was certain Sloan was unaware of his mother's look.

Myron Whittaker returned with champagne and several glasses. A great production was made out of opening the bottle. Laughter filled the room as the bubbling brew foamed onto the rug.

Joy accepted the glass and stood stiffly apart from the cozy family scene by the fireplace hearth. Her smile was strained, but when Sloan's father offered a toast her response was genuine. She smiled warmly at Sloan, afraid her heart was in her eyes. Then purposefully she looked down into the sparkling liquid before taking a sip.

"This is fantastic," Sloan said, and reached for the half-empty bottle.

"California, of course," Myron Whittaker bragged. "Some of the world's finest is grown right here."

"Honestly, dear, you sound like an advertisement."

Watching the small family interact naturally with one another produced an ache Joy knew she would endure for years hereafter. She would never fit into this family, with their wealth and position. It wasn't difficult to tell that Sloan's parents were concerned with their son's obvious attraction to her. And with good cause, Joy acknowledged.

"We must have a party." Margaret Whittaker's words broke into Joy's troubled musings. "Invite all your old friends."

Joy could almost visualize all the wheels turning in his mother's head.

"Here, of course," she continued. "It'll be easier for you that way. We'll invite the Jordans and the Baxters and the Reagans and the Considines."

"Mother." Sloan's sharp tone caused Margaret Whittaker to pause.

"Yes, dear?"

"There will be no party."

"Of course there will. You've been out of circulation for months. People are beginning to ask questions."

"Let them. There will be no party," he repeated forcefully.

"But Sloan." His mother's eyes were soft and pleading. Joy didn't know how anyone could refuse her, and sincerely doubted that it happened often.

"I'm tired. Joy," he called for her, and held out his arm. "Help me back to my room."

Joy set her nearly full wineglass down on an end table and strode across the suddenly silent area.

"Don't say it," Sloan murmured as they reached his room and he lowered his weight in the wheelchair.

"Say what?" Joy asked, pretending not to know.

"For most of my life I've fallen into Mother's schemes, but not anymore. I have nothing in common with the Baxters, or any of those people."

Joy straightened, standing in the doorway, one hand braced against the wooden frame. "Don't look at me. That's your decision."

"Then why do I feel so damn guilty?" He slammed his fist against the rubber wheel.

"Parents do have the knack of doing that to us sometimes."

Sloan whipped a hand across his face. "I mean what I say, and Mother knows that. It'll be interesting to see what lengths she'll be willing to go to get her own way. I love my mother, but I'm not a fool."

It didn't take even twenty-four hours for Joy to learn exactly what Margaret Whittaker had in mind. Mid-morning, Clara handed Joy a phone message that asked Joy to meet Margaret Whittaker in the best restaurant in Oxnard for lunch. Joy dreaded the confrontation.

"You look nice," Sloan commented as she brought in his lunch tray. "Where are you headed?"

"I have an appointment in town."

"Oh?" He arched one thick brow curiously. When Joy didn't elaborate, he continued. "Anyone I know?"

"Honestly, who said I was meeting anyone? It could be with the dentist." Over the years Joy had gained a certain amount of poise. She didn't want to mislead Sloan; nor did she wish to cause ill will between mother and son.

"What time will you be back?" he questioned further.

"You're beginning to sound like my guardian," she accused teasingly with an underlying tone of seriousness.

Sloan reached out and took her hand, squeezing it lovingly. Even his lightest touch was enough to cause chaos with her emotions. A tingling awareness spread up her arm. "That's the last way I want you to think of me." He smiled at her, his voice deep and calm while his eyes shone into hers.

Joy nodded and backed away. The need to escape was growing to the point of desperation. If she couldn't disguise her feelings for him, then everything would be lost and she would have to leave.

Margaret Whittaker was already seated when Joy arrived.

"My dear, how nice of you to come."

"How thoughtful of you to invite me," Joy murmured, hating small talk and knowing she would be forced to endure at least an hour of it until Sloan's mother came to the point of the meeting.

The waitress arrived, filled Joy's water glass, and handed her a menu. Joy ordered almost without looking. She doubted that she'd be able to choke down anything more than a salad. Already she could feel the sensitive muscles of her stomach tighten.

"Such lovely weather this time of year, don't you agree?" Sloan's mother murmured the question.

"Yes." Joy nodded. Her right hand surrounded the water glass, collecting the condensation. "May is my favorite month."

"You've done remarkably well with Sloan."

"Thank you."

"Believe me when I say I know how difficult he can be."

"He was in the beginning, but came to accept me shortly afterwards."

"How much longer will it be before Sloan's completely independent?"

"A few weeks, not much more than that." She swallowed a sip of ice water. It slid down her throat, easing the building tightness.

"One of the reasons I invited you here today is to ask about Sloan's social readjustment. I'm sure you've dealt with situations like this before."

Joy hadn't, but didn't say so. "I believe that, given time, Sloan will readjust automatically."

"I had so hoped he would agree to the party. He knows how much I love parties, and everyone has been so concerned. It seems like such a good way to help my son. Don't you agree?"

"I really couldn't say, Mrs. Whittaker." Uncomfortable, Joy lowered her gaze. So this was the reason Margaret Whittaker had invited her to lunch.

"Has he mentioned the party to you?"

"Not since yesterday."

"What did he say then?" the older woman probed.

"Mrs. Whittaker, please," Joy said, and breathed in softly. "I don't think it's my place to relay your son's feelings."

"But I had so hoped." She gave Joy a softly pleading glance, not unlike the one Joy had witnessed her giving Sloan.

The waitress arrived with their salads. Joy smiled her thanks and lifted the fork. She didn't need to take a bite to know the meal would taste like overcooked mush.

"I think that if you talked to Sloan..." Margaret Whittaker continued, her gaze centered on the meal. "What I mean to say is that I've noticed the way my son looks at you."

Joy's heart leaped into her throat. "What do you mean?"

"It's only natural that Sloan would feel a certain amount of gratitude toward you. He respects and likes you. If you were to ask him about the party, I'm sure he would agree. Won't you, dear?" she quizzed softly. "For Sloan's sake?"

Eight

Joy laid the fork beside her untouched salad. "I sincerely doubt that my asking will have any effect on Sloan's decision."

"But you will try?" Margaret Whittaker entreated.

"Yes," Joy agreed, nodding with reluctant capitulation, when what she wanted was to keep Sloan to herself for the rest of her life.

As Joy returned to the beach house, she knew what she had to do. Sloan's mother had made the position clear. Joy's responsibilities went far beyond the physical therapy Sloan required. He was almost to the point of walking on his own now. Her last duty would be to bring him back into the mainstream of life.

Hands clenching the steering wheel, Joy drove to the shoulder of the highway and stopped completely. The scenery was spectacular. Huge waves pounded the rocky shoreline. Large gulls swooped low in a sky that was cloudless. Heaving a sigh, Joy lowered her face until her brow pressed against her coiled hands. A building moistness clouded her eyes as she struggled for control. What Margaret Whittaker was really asking was that Joy relinquish her love. Of course, she had been subtle, but genuinely concerned that Sloan fit back into the lifestyle he had known before the accident. One that excluded Joy.

Sloan was in the hallway when Joy rounded the corner, eager to escape to her room unseen. She stopped abruptly when she saw him.

Large-knuckled hands gripped the walker. Slowly Joy raised her eyes to meet his.

"How was your appointment?"

"Fine."

A smiling knowledge lurked behind his dark eyes. "You don't look pleased about it. What's the matter, did the dentist find a cavity?"

"I wasn't at the dentist."

His mouth curved in a smile, the look deliberately casual. "I suppose my mother's been at it again."

Joy attempted to disguise her startled expression. "How'd you know where I was?"

"I didn't. But I happen to know my mother. I didn't think she'd let this party thing drop so easily." He shifted his weight, and Joy recognized that he was getting tired.

"Go back to your room and I'll bring us coffee."

Readily Sloan agreed, and Joy returned a few minutes later with a full pot and two cups.

When Sloan saw the tray he lifted one dark brow. "You expect this is going to take a while?" The look he gave her was both amused and curious.

"It could," Joy responded noncommittally.

Her hand shook a little as she poured a cup and handed it to Sloan.

"You are nervous." The sharp gaze followed her movements.

"Not really," she said, attempting to smooth over her telltale trembling. With her cup resting on her knee, Joy sat across from Sloan, who was at his desk.

"All right, let's have it. What's Mother said to you?"

"Nothing so terrible."

"I can imagine."

"Don't," Joy said quickly in defense of the older woman. "You've spent a hellish nine months; I don't think you realize how hard this has been on your parents."

His mouth narrowed slightly. "I admit things haven't been easy for any of us."

"Now that you're walking again, your mother needs the assurance that things are going to be the same."

Sloan rubbed his hands together, the movement marked with frustration. "I'm not the man I was nine months ago."

"You are and you aren't," Joy murmured, staring into the steaming black liquid.

Sloan's frown was curious.

"In some ways you can't change," Joy continued. "Certainly not who or what you are. But you're bound to see things differently. Life is suddenly precious, and what was once important means nothing." She sat awkwardly on the edge of the straightbacked chair. "I don't know if any of this makes sense."

"It makes perfect sense. That's exactly how I feel."

"The struggles, the pain, have made you…"

"Us," he interrupted, immediately linking them together.

"Us," she added, and swallowed. The tightness in her throat was mounting until it felt as if someone's hands were around her neck in a stranglehold. "I know how it was with me. My whole world revolved around my family. I felt secure with them. I didn't want to face the world. People can be cruel, and I wasn't sure I could handle it if someone saw my scars." Her voice contained the rawness of remembered pain, but she continued steady and even. "Now that time has come for you too."

"Or so my mother says," Sloan murmured dryly.

"And I agree."

"Has it come down to taking sides?"

"I hoped it wouldn't."

"Apparently, Mother's conned you into believing this party idea of hers will bring me back into the social circle?" His tone was cynical.

"Your mother hasn't conned me into anything. She's concerned and wants what's best for you."

"And has appointed herself as my guardian to issue me back into a life I want to leave dead and buried."

Joy's smile was crooked and filled with amusement.

"You find this situation comical?"

"No." She shook her head while her finger absently made a circular motion around the top of the cup. "You remind me so much of myself. The thing is, Sloan, as much as you'd like to remain a hermit in this beautiful retreat, there's a whole world waiting for you."

He emitted a harsh, bitter sound that Joy chose to ignore.

"The point of everything is that I believe your mother may not be so far off base with this party idea. For weeks now, I've watched you build a fortress against the outside world. The time has come to face these doubts straight on."

He was silent, intense, and to all appearances hadn't heard a word she'd said. "You're asking me to let my mother go ahead with the plans for this party."

"Yes." Her voice was raw and faintly husky.

Sloan closed his eyes and uttered a low, frustrated groan. "Damn her." He slammed his hand against the top of the desk, shooting papers in every direction.

Joy gasped, and her hand flew to her breast.

His mouth pinched tight, Sloan's head bobbed in cynical acknowledgement. "She knew the only person in the world I'd do this for was you."

"It's got to be for you, Sloan." If they didn't end the conversation soon, Joy was convinced she'd break into tears.

Margaret Whittaker couldn't possibly understand what she had asked of Joy. Not only must she relinquish her love, but she must give Sloan back to a life he claimed he didn't want.

"All right." Sloan ran a hand along the side of his head, smoothing the dark hair. "I'll call Mother and tell her I'll agree to this stupid party."

"Thank you." Joy stood before a sob escaped and humiliated her. "I'm sure you won't regret it."

"I already do." Sloan's muttered words followed her out of the room.

The party plans were set for the following weekend. Clara couldn't hope to manage everything, and extra help was brought in. Margaret Whittaker became a permanent fixture, bustling in and out, a flurry of activity following her wherever she went. The house, staff, everyone was thrown into an unbelievable tizzy.

As much as possible, Joy stayed out of the way. Tuesday she phoned Danielle to see if there was a possibility of their getting together that Saturday night, but Danielle had already made plans. Not wishing to involve herself, Joy decided to spend the night at her apartment and return the following Sunday morning.

Sloan joined her on the verandah the night before the planned gala event. He stopped his walker beside her and waited until she'd finished playing the musical score on the flute.

"Do you see what you've done?" he teased, referring to the party.

"Does your mother do everything like this?"

"Everything," Sloan confirmed with a chuckle. "But I admit this one tops the cake. I think Dad nearly had a stroke when Mother insisted on new carpeting in the living room."

"I hope you don't mind if I slip out early tomorrow afternoon—" She wasn't allowed to finish.

"Slip out!" he repeated angrily.

"Yes, I thought I'd spend the night at my apartment. You don't need—" Again she was interrupted.

"Don't need!" he shouted unreasonably. "Listen here. It's because of you that I agreed to this whole thing. I have no intention of letting you get out of it."

"But I can't go."

"What the blazes do you mean by that?"

Not for weeks had Joy seen Sloan so angry. "I . . . I don't belong there."

"The only reason I agreed to this fiasco was that I assumed you'd be with me."

"But, Sloan, these are your friends. I won't know anyone."

"You'll know me."

A feeling of desolation stole over her. "But I don't have anything to wear to something like this."

"Take tomorrow off and buy yourself a dress," he shot back.

"It doesn't matter what I say. You have an answer." Her chin jutted out defiantly.

"You're right. And you'd better decide soon. Otherwise this whole affair's going to be canceled."

Nervously Joy trailed her fingers along the railing. "But I don't want to go. I'll stick out like a sore thumb."

Sloan's sharp laughter filled the night. "And you think I won't? There's no way I'll endure tomorrow without you. Now, do you agree, or will I be forced to start a war within my own family?"

The soft line of her mouth thinned angrily. "I don't like this, Sloan Whittaker. I don't like it one bit."

L.J. offered some comfort early the next morning when Joy walked along the sandy beach and plopped down on a log. With short strokes, Joy smoothed the gull's feathers down the back of his head.

"It isn't working like I'd planned," she complained. "Not at all."

L.J. cocked his head undisturbed. A few other gulls flew overhead and landed down the beach. L.J.'s interest peaked as he squawked loudly. The returning sounds seemed to excite him, and he scurried toward his friends, his feet leaving wet indentations in the sand.

Joy's heart plummeted to her feet as she watched the bird she had come to love hurry away. Would she lose him? L.J. was tame now, at least for her. Would he fit back into the life he had left? She was almost glad when he turned around and hobbled back to her side. The gauze that held his wing against his body was what restrained him. Joy knew she shouldn't be glad, but she was.

The remainder of the morning and all afternoon was spent shopping. Joy gave up counting the number of dresses she tried on. By afternoon she was weak with worry. It didn't matter what she wore; nothing could change what she was: somewhat plain, short, and scarred.

The dress she finally chose was made of pink crepe with simple but elegant lines. The belt contained a white rose pin. By the time she made her decision, Joy had given up caring. The sales clerk told her it was lovely, but Joy didn't doubt that the woman was prompted by the thought of a big sale. The hairdresser styled her short hair in bouncy curls that made her look like the comic strip character Betty Boop. Joy washed it out when she got home.

Sloan was nowhere in sight, and Joy stayed in her room, preferring not to interfere with everything that was going on around the house.

The knock on her bedroom door surprised her. She stood, running a light hand over the long pink skirt before answering.

Sloan, dressed in a dark suit and tie, stood supported by crutches outside her door. The sight of this virile, handsome man was enough to steal her breath. His smile was devilishly enticing and slashed deep grooves around his mouth. His dancing dark eyes were directed at her and slowly took in every inch of her appearance. Apparently, what he saw pleased him, as an immense look of satisfaction showed in his eyes.

"Will I do?" The words stuck in her throat and sounded almost scratchy.

His answering nod was absent. "I see you every day in your white uniform. Sometimes, on the weekends, in your cords and jeans. But this is the first time I've ever seen you all dressed up."

"I feel like a fish out of water."

"And you look like a princess. My Joy, you are a beautiful woman." He said it as if it surprised him.

The color invading her face seeped up from her neck. "And you, Sloan Whittaker, bear a striking resemblance to Prince Charming."

"So it's been said," he teased. "Shall we?" He proffered his elbow. Joy rested her hand lightly against the crook of his arm and inhaled a deep breath, readying herself for the ordeal.

"I'll be the envy of every man here," he whispered reassuringly, and paused in the hallway just out of view from the living room. "Relax. You're as stiff as starched underwear."

Under any other circumstances Joy would have laughed, but she felt like a coiled spring, her nerves in chaos.

"Joy." Her name was issued on a soft reassuring note. The gentle brush of his lips on her cheek sent a warm glow over her. "Now smile."

She painted one on her lips and prayed it would effectively disguise her nervousness.

People had already begun to arrive. Joy didn't know a soul, not even the help who sauntered in and around the guests with trays of drinks and hors d'oeuvres.

Filled with her own insecurities, Joy had forgotten what an ordeal this was for Sloan. She glanced at him, a protective spark burning in her eyes.

Sloan's mother was at their side the minute they stepped into the room. Dressed in a lovely silver creation, she looked years younger. Diamonds graced her neck and arms. The scent of gardenias followed her.

"Ladies and gentleman," Margaret Whittaker announced solemnly, "the guest of honor, my son Sloan."

Sloan tossed his mother a look of severe displeasure, but graciously smiled at the small audience.

A flurry of introductions followed, for Joy's benefit. After five minutes she gave up trying to remember names and faces.

A path was cleared for Sloan as he purposefully made his way into the room. He chose a far corner chair and set the crutches at his side.

"Joy," he whispered tightly. "Get me something to drink. I'm going to need it."

Joy felt exactly the opposite. More than at any time she could remember, she needed her wits about her. But getting something non-alcoholic in this crowd might be impossible.

A waiter was readily available. Joy lifted a long-stemmed wineglass from the silver tray. "Would it be possible to have a Coke or something?"

"Right away, madame."

Joy relaxed somewhat. Maybe this wouldn't be as bad as she had assumed. Sloan took the wineglass out of her hand and placed an arm around her waist.

"Sit here." He indicated the padded arm of the chair. When she did as he requested, Sloan kept his hand where it was. Joy knew she should object. The reason for this gathering was to bring Sloan back into contact with his friends—and that included women.

Joy spotted Trixie a few minutes later. Blonde. Beautiful. Perfect. Everything Joy would never be. Trixie laid a thin cobwebbed lace shawl over Clara's arm and smiled beguilingly into a tall man's eyes. Obviously her date. Joy relaxed.

"What was that for?" Sloan asked, his hand tightening possessively around her.

"What?"

"That sigh," he returned.

"Trixie's here."

"Joy whatever you do, don't leave me."

"Sloan?" She couldn't understand him.

"Don't 'Sloan' me. I want you here as protection."

"I'm your nurse, not your armed guard," she shot back hotly. Silently she gritted her teeth.

"Joy," he whispered entreatingly. "If someone makes one condescending remark or patronizes me, I won't be responsible for my actions. I need you as a buffer."

"A pillow would have done as well. Why drag me into this when you know how much I hate it? Haven't you any consideration for someone other than yourself?"

"Hello, Sloan." It was the man who had come in with Trixie. He stood directly in front of them.

"Dale." The greeting was sadly lacking in warmth. "Forgive me for not standing up," Sloan mocked.

"That I can overlook. It's the constant brush-off you've been giving me these past months I'm having a hard time forgiving."

"I'd think after the first few times you would have gotten the message."

Dale directed his attention to Joy. "Since Sloan is delinquent in introducing us, I'll do it myself. I'm Dale Jewett, Sloan's friend, although that at the moment is questionable."

"How do you do," Joy responded primly. So this was the man Sloan had repeatedly sent away.

"I think there's something you should understand right now." Sloan's voice was coated in ice. "My tennis days are over, skiing no longer appeals to me, and my golf game is shot."

Dale laughed and loudly slapped his knee. "You mean that's what's been bugging you all these months? Do you think I care if you can do any of that?"

Joy slid off the seat. Sloan had released his hold, and didn't seem to notice that she'd moved. "If you'll excuse me a minute."

Sloan didn't answer. Joy stepped aside and watched as Dale pulled up the ottoman and sat down. Within seconds the two men were engrossed in conversation.

The waiter delivered her Coke, and Joy stood in the background. Someone she vaguely remembered being introduced to engaged her in a conversation, but Joy was only half listening, making monosyllabic responses when required. Apparently the woman was a distant cousin of the Whittakers and had heard all kinds of good things about Joy from another cousin.

Dale was joined by Trixie, who proudly held out her left hand. A solitaire diamond sparkled from her ring finger. Joy felt like jumping up and down and applauding. She watched as the two men enthusiastically shook hands.

Sloan turned and started to say something, unaware she had left. His eyes briefly scanned the crowd until they fell on her. They narrowed slightly before indicating he wanted her.

"Excuse me, please," Joy told the friendly cousin. The Coke glass in her hand, she sauntered back to Sloan's side.

"You rang, Master?" she teased.

His arm came around her waist. "The funny-girl is Joy."

"We've met," both Trixie and Dale said at the same time, and laughed. The two were so obviously in love that Joy instantly shared in their happiness.

"From what I understand, you're the one responsible for this minor miracle."

"No, the credit goes to Sloan. The only praise I can accept is being tenacious enough to stick it out with him."

"This little lady pinched, poked, prodded, and punished me."

"All in the line of duty," Joy joked.

"Sometimes above-and-beyond duties call," Sloan inserted dramatically.

Another couple joined them. Again Joy was introduced, his hand at her waist keeping her possessively at his side. When he handed her his empty glass, Joy stood to go refill it for him.

Dale had broken through the brick wall that Sloan had erected, and now the sounds of his laughter could be heard above the rest. The crowd around him had grown so large that Joy didn't bother to push her way through.

"Didn't I tell you what a good idea this party was?" Margaret Whittaker brushed past, cheerful and happy, "Myron and I couldn't be more pleased with everything you've done."

She held the fragile stem of Sloan's drink with both hands. "Thank you," she murmured humbly.

"We'd like to give you a generous bonus." Her husband had mentioned the same thing once before. Joy didn't want a reward. It was enough that she had accomplished what she set out to do.

"Really, Mrs. Whittaker, that won't be necessary."

"Of course it's necessary. Now don't argue."

Joy was quickly learning that the Whittakers were accustomed to having things their own way. It wouldn't do her any good to disagree.

Myron joined his wife, his hand cupping her shoulder. "Good evening, Miss Nielsen."

"Hello, Mr. Whittaker."

"Are you enjoying yourself?"

"Very much." The lie was only a white one.

"Juliette's here." The words were directed to his wife.

Margaret was instantly alert. "Do you think inviting her was wise?" A curious note of concern entered her voice. "Juliette and Sloan were quite serious before the accident," the older woman explained.

"Oh." Joy struggled to sound as natural as possible.

"I'm so hoping they get back together again."

A swirling nausea attacked Joy.

"They were always so perfect for one another."

"What happened?" Joy wanted a reason to hate the mysterious Juliette. Had the woman walked out on him after the accident?

"All Sloan's doing, I fear. He didn't want anyone around. I'm afraid he hurt her terribly."

"Don't worry, dear," Myron Whittaker commented. "I'm sure now that Sloan's walking they'll patch things up."

"What has been your experience in cases like this?" Margaret asked. Both parents looked to Joy.

She forced a reassuring smile. "I really couldn't say."

A middle-aged woman came up and whispered something in Myron's ear. He nodded.

"Miss Nielsen, would you mind checking with Clara in the kitchen. It seems we've run out of hors d'oeuvres."

"Of course not."

Her nerves felt raw as she sauntered into the kitchen. Clara was busy working, placing large shrimp onto a silver platter.

"How's it going in here?"

Clara looked up, startled. "My goodness, what are you doing in here, child?"

"Mr. Whittaker sent me to see how the goodies are holding out."

"What he really wants to know is if the little pink fellows have made their debut yet." She held up a shrimp.

"I guess you could say that." A smile touched the edge of her mouth.

"Tell him to hold his horses, for heaven's sake. There's only so much these old fingers of mine can do."

"All right, I'll tell him. But if you don't mind, I'll use more delicate terms."

Clara's look was perplexed, her brow knit in deep creases. "Now scat before something spills on that pretty dress."

Sloan's wineglass was still in her hand as she returned to the party. The Whittakers were out of sight, and Joy suspected Myron had purposely sent her away in order to bring Juliette to Sloan's attention. It was probably best. Joy didn't want to meet someone that was perfect for him.

"There you are." Trixie stepped to her side. "Sloan sent me to find you."

Joy took in a breath to make her voice sound calm. "I imagine he's ready for his drink. I got waylaid."

"His drink?" Trixie returned hesitantly. "No, Dale got him a refill earlier. Sloan wants you."

What lovely words, Joy mused as she followed the blonde through the crowd.

Several people were standing in front of Sloan, some leaning against the furniture, drinks in hand, a friendly crowd that responded with laughing eagerness to his witticisms. The attention didn't bother him, but unnerved her.

Their eyes met and Joy stopped midstep. She didn't want to be thrust into the middle of this, and silently she relayed as much. Her hands balled into tight fists as she stood outside the circle of friends. She didn't belong here, and he knew it.

Someone whispered Juliette's name, and Joy's attention was diverted to another blonde who moved gracefully across the room toward Sloan.

A hush fell over the crowd.

"Hello, Sloan," the husky-pitched voice purred seductively.

Joy couldn't listen, couldn't watch. Abruptly she turned away and for a timeless second was frozen into immobility as the warm sound of Sloan's welcome reached her.

Somehow she made it back to her room, which felt stifling and hot. The sliding-glass door made a grating noise as she opened it and stepped onto the verandah. Arms hugging her waist, Joy raised her face to the heavens, blinking back the ready tears. Almost from the time she'd arrived, she'd known this would happen. There was no one to blame but herself. She was the foolish one to have given her heart to Sloan Whittaker.

Tonight had magnified their differences. From the moment she'd stepped into the room it had been apparent she didn't belong. Sloan's world was light years away from anything she'd ever known. He was accustomed to wealth, influential people, and a certain amount of power.

Her job was almost complete, and she couldn't be anything but happy with how things had worked out. Her heart, however, was weeping for the man who had cried out for her in his sleep. But he was lost to her forever.

"I thought I'd find you here," Sloan spoke from behind.

"You should be with your guests," she mumbled, not turning.

"Why didn't you come back?"

She could hear the sound of his crutches as he moved closer to her side.

Tension crackled in the space separating them.

"I couldn't." Her weak voice was barely audible.

"That's not an answer."

"All right, I don't belong in there. Is that what you want me to say? Because it's true." Her lower lip quivered traitorously.

"Don't give me that garbage." The angry words exploded into the still night. A hand on her shoulder turned her around.

Joy hung her head, not wanting him to see the tears that brimmed, ready to spill down her pale cheek. "How's Juliette?"

"Fine. We didn't talk long. I was too eager to find you." A hand stroked the slender curve of her neck and down her shoulder. The other found its way to the back of her neck. A fiery warmth rushed down her spine. "How long is it going to take you to learn that the two of us belong together? We're a team."

The pressure of his hands brought her up onto her tiptoes.

"Don't," she pleaded, and her voice trembled. "Sloan, I can't bear it. Please don't."

His hand closed more firmly around her neck, bringing her against the solid wall of his chest. "Don't you know yet how much I love you?" His voice was incredibly gentle, caressing her upturned face.

Agony was tearing at her heart. "You can't love me."

"But I do." His mouth moved against her hair in a rough action. The heat of his body burned through the flimsy material of her dress. His heartbeat hammered erratically against her palm.

For a moment she managed to elude his searching kiss, but when his mouth found hers, all protest died. She wound her arms around his neck and gave herself completely to his probing kiss. Everything went spinning, a magical merry-go-round that ascended to dizzying heights. Feeling boneless, she molded her body to his. Sloan had once said that they fit perfectly together. For the first time, she was able to test how accurate his statement was.

"Come on, my Joy," he whispered against her nape. "As much as I want to stay here and hold you the rest of our lives, we have to go back." He chuckled softly. "At this point, it would be best to avoid Mother's wrath."

Nine

Joy sat on a burned-out log along the beach. Her flute lay across her lap and L.J. hobbled about her feet. The early morning air contained a crisp chill, but Joy was only vaguely aware of her surroundings.

"I should be the happiest woman in the world," she told the attentive gull. "Sloan said he loved me last night." She raised the flute to her lips and played a few mournful notes. "Talk to me, L.J. Tell me why I feel so miserable."

The bird looked back at her blankly.

"Come on," Joy moaned regretfully. "This isn't doing any good. Let's go back."

She stood and continued to play as she walked along the sand-covered shore, L.J. trailing behind. Once she glanced back, and a smile lit up her face. She felt like a pied piper.

When the house came into view, she noted that Sloan was standing on the verandah, looking out. She paused and waved. He returned the gesture, but even from this distance she could see that something was bothering him.

He was still outside when she put L.J. back into the fenced yard and returned to her room. She carelessly laid the flute across the mattress and joined Sloan on the wooden deck.

"What's wrong?"

He glared at her for a moment, his look thoughtful. "I didn't know you still had the bird."

"He's just like a pet now."

"The two of you made quite a pair walking on the beach like that." Somehow he didn't sound like it was a pleasant sight.

"Something's troubling you. What is it, Sloan?" She placed her hand on his forearm, and he covered it with his own.

"You say the bird is tame. For everyone?"

"No, only me. But I was the one who treated him and I'm the one who feeds him."

"Hasn't he ever given any indication he wants to be free?"

"No..." She stopped, remembering his reaction the other day when some gulls were
near.

"I notice his wing is still bandaged. I'd think
by now it would be healed."

Joy straightened her back and took a step in
retreat. "What you're suggesting is that the
time has come to set the bird free." She struggled to take the protest out of her words.

"I know how you feel about him."

"You couldn't possibly know. I found him;
I was the one who took care of him. He eats
right out of my hand now. He's tame, I tell
you. He doesn't want his freedom; he's content to stay here." Her voice became thinner
with every word as she argued.

"You're right," Sloan reasoned. "The bird
is yours; you're the one who worked with him.
I'm just asking that you think about it."

Joy tried to smile, but the effort resulted in
a mere trembling of her mouth. Swallowing
back a sob, she squared her shoulders. "I think
you're right. L.J. deserves a better life than
this." Abruptly she turned around, intent on
doing it while the strength of her conviction
remained strong.

"Where are you going?"

"To set L.J. free."

"It doesn't have to be done now."

"Yes, it does." Unreasonably, she felt like shouting at him.

Her mouth was set in a firm, unyielding line as she marched down to the back portion of the yard and opened the gate. She didn't need to say a word for the gull to come rushing out. Like a tiny robot, he followed her down to the beach.

Tears blurred her eyes as she knelt at his side and unwrapped the gauze bandage from his wing. Carefully she extended it, checking for any further damage. There wasn't anything that she could see.

"We've become good friends over the last few weeks, haven't we, Long John?"

He tested his new freedom, then quirked his small head at an inquiring angle when he experienced the first unruffling of his broad wingspan.

Joy bit into the corner of her bottom lip at the happy squawk he gave.

"The time has come for you to go back to your other friends." Her voice was incredibly weak.

The bird continued to stare back at her.

"Go on," she urged. "Fly away. Scat."

He didn't budge.

"Sloan's right," she spoke in a whisper. "He told me it was time to set you free." Joy choked on a sob. "But it wasn't you he was talking about. Sloan's ready too."

"Long John," she groaned. "This is hard enough without your making it any more painful." She rose and brushed the sand from her pants. "You're free. Go."

Still he didn't move.

Joy began to run, and to her horror the bird followed behind as he'd done so many times in the past.

"No." She shouted and waved her hands in an effort to frighten him away.

He looked at her as if he were laughing.

She picked up a pebble and tossed it at him. It bounced a few inches away.

He let out an angry squawk.

"Go," she shouted with all her strength. Just when it didn't look as if anything she did would make any difference, another gull swooped onto the beach.

"Your friends are here," she told him in a gentle voice that probably confused him all the more. "Go to them. It's where you belong."

He glanced from her to the sky. Testing his wing a second time, he rose and hovered in the air above her. He seemed reluctant to go.

Standing completely still, Joy placed a hand over her mouth and raised the other in a final salute to the bird she had come to love. Burning tears streamed down her cheek.

Her heart breaking, she stayed on the shore until he was out of sight. She turned, and the beach house loomed before her.

Almost from the beginning she had found similarities between Sloan and L.J. They were two of a kind. In the beginning each had been arrogant and proud. She had been the one to tame them, and she must be the one to set them free. The decision was long overdue. Sloan didn't need her anymore. Within a matter of days he'd be able to go from the walker to the cane. Why had she waited? It only made the parting more painful.

Her lower lip trembling, Joy returned to the house. Mercifully Clara wasn't in the kitchen, and Joy hurried down the hall to her room. The suitcases were under the bed, and she knelt down to pull them out.

The first thing she packed was her flute in the small black carrying case that resembled a doctor's bag. Without rhyme or order she began tossing her things inside the open bags.

When the largest one was filled, she dragged it off the bed and out of the house. Somehow she managed to get it into the back of her car. An acid tear weaved a crooked path down one cheek, and Joy paused to wipe it aside. This was going to be difficult enough without adding more emotion to it.

Sloan was in the hallway outside her bedroom when she returned. Without a word, she scooted past him.

"What are you doing?"

"Packing."

He laughed. "You're kidding."

"No," she said forcefully, "I'm not."

"You can't mean it." He sounded shocked.

"Isn't it obvious?" she returned flatly. "Look in my room. My bags are out; my clothes are on the bed. To put it plain and simple, I'm leaving."

"But why? I don't understand."

Holding her expression tight, Joy released an impatient sigh. "What's there to understand? My job is finished. You're up and around. That's what I came here for. Now it's time to move on." She strived to sound as un emotional as possible.

She saw his hands tighten around the metal bar that supported him. "It's that damn bird, isn't it?"

"Of course not."

"I knew the minute you left that something was wrong. Let's talk about it, at least. Don't just walk out."

"Mr. Whittaker." Clara ambled down the hall. "I haven't seen Joy this morning."

"She's here," he replied, obviously irritated by the interruption.

"But she didn't bring you breakfast or nothing."

"She claims she's leaving," Sloan announced, and his mouth compressed into a thin line.

"No." Clara emphatically shook her head to deny the truth. "Joy wouldn't leave without saying something. That's not like her."

Joy came through the doorway carrying as much as possible under both arms. Only one suitcase remained. "I was coming back to say good-bye to you and Paul."

"But not me?" His look cut her to the quick.

She didn't answer him.

"Joy." Frustration coated his voice as he stepped aside to allow her to pass. "Why are you doing this?"

"Because I have to, don't you see?"

"No, I don't," he shouted angrily.

Joy hurried out of the house and threw her things into the car. She paused long enough to take in several deep, calming breaths.

Clara was standing in the front doorway, her brown face tight with concern. "What's happened?"

"Nothing." Joy attempted to brush away the housekeeper's doubts. "The time has come for me to leave, that's all. You knew from the beginning I would go."

"But not like this, so sudden and all."

"Sometimes it's better that way. Clara, you've been a dear. I'll never forget you." Briefly she hugged the warm, generous woman. "Where's Paul?"

"He's gone into town," Clara replied, her look preoccupied.

"Then give him my best. I can't wait."

"Why can't you?" Clara demanded in uncharacteristic sharpness.

Joy didn't answer; instead she stepped back into the house and headed straight to her room. Sloan was inside waiting for her. He slammed the door shut after she entered.

Hands clenched, Joy whirled on him. "Why'd you do that?"

"I'll lock you in here until hell freezes over if you don't tell me what's going on."

"What's there to explain? The time has come for me to take on another case, that's all."

"But I need you."

"Nonsense. Everything I do, Paul can do," she explained tersely.

"That's not it, and you know it."

Her chin jutted out in challenge. "I know nothing of the sort." Her hand closed around the suitcase handle as she lifted it off the bed.

"Doesn't last night mean anything to you?"

Joy's greatest fear was that he would bring up his love. Silently she prayed God would give her strength. "Of course it does. But those feelings of gratitude are common—" She wasn't allowed to finish.

"It isn't gratitude." He was angry and shouting. "What does it take to reach you?"

With the suitcase in her hand, she stalked across the floor.

"Don't walk out on me, Joy, or you'll regret it."

A sad smile briefly touched her mouth; she would regret this day all her life. Slowly, she turned to face him. "Good-bye, Sloan. May God grant you a rich and full life." Her own would be empty and desolate. Tears clouded her eyes as she turned around, her back to him, one hand on the door.

"Don't leave me. Not like this." A wealth of emotion filled Sloan's plea.

The temptation to turn around and run into his arms was so strong that Joy felt as if she were fighting an invisible force that was pulling her apart.

"Good-bye," she repeated, her voice trembling and weak.

Something exploded behind her. Joy swung around just in time to see Sloan hurl a vase against the opposite wall. It shattered into a hundred pieces.

"Get out," he shouted, knocking the bedside lamp aside. "You're right. I don't need you. Get out of my life and stay out." Defiance glared from his dark eyes.

All color drained out of her face as she stood frozen and immobile.

"What are you waiting for? Do I have to kick you out the door?" He took the walker and slammed it against the dresser. "I don't need you. Understand?"

Joy understood all too well. Swallowing, she walked out of the room. Her legs felt as if they could buckle under her, but somehow she managed.

Clara stood in the entryway, wringing her hands. "Sure gonna miss you around here. Won't seem like the same place with you gone."

"Thank you, Clara." Tears ran freely down her face. "Take care of him for me." Her voice was breaking, and she paused to take in a breath, then tilted her head toward Sloan's room so Clara would know what she meant.

"I will, but it's you he needs."

"He'll be fine."

"But will you?"

The confirming nod was weak. "I think so."

Without looking back, Joy walked out of the house, climbed in her car, started the engine, and pulled away.

* * *

"I won't do any more private cases," Joy emphasized as she spoke into the telephone receiver. She knew that Dr. Phelps was upset with her, but Joy had learned her lesson. Never again.

"You're sure? The money is good," Dr. Phelps persisted.

"The money is always good."

"You did a fabulous job with Whittaker."

"Thank you." Joy bit her lip to keep from asking how he was. Three weeks had seemed more like three years.

"I understand you're working at the Sports Clinic now."

"Yes, I started a couple of weeks ago."

"How do you like it?"

Joy couldn't very well admit it was boring, unchallenging, and that every day away from Sloan she was dying a little more. "It's regular hours, no hassles and . . ."

"Crummy pay," Dr. Phelps finished for her.

"And that," she agreed with a weak laugh.

"I can't talk you into this case?"

"No, I'm afraid not."

"Should I try again?"

"You can try, but I doubt if I'll change my mind." She knew Dr. Phelps was disappointed in her. "I'm sorry," she murmured, and replaced the receiver.

Her hand rested on top of the phone. No less than twenty times after she'd left Sloan, she'd been tempted to call and see how things were going. The only thing that had stopped her was the fear that Sloan would answer. Some nights she had lain awake and allowed her mind to play back the memories. They'd shared some happy times, good times. Her favorite had been when they'd sat on the beach, Sloan at her side, his hands fingering her hair.

So many times they'd sat on the verandah late at night and discussed a myriad of subjects. Amazingly, their tastes and opinions were often similar.

Joy hadn't expected to miss his companionship so much, nor his friendship. Sloan had been her friend, a very good friend.

A long sigh escaped her as she tucked her feet under her in the big overstuffed chair. Joy rested her head against the back cushion and closed her eyes. Three weeks, and she'd yet to sleep an entire night through. She felt exhausted and frustrated with herself.

The decision had been the right one. Both times. L.J. was free to join his own kind and live the life he was meant to. Just as Sloan was now. She would no more fit in Sloan's world than she would in L.J.'s. For a time they would miss her. It would be a natural reaction. But later those feelings would change. Soon, if not already, Sloan would realize she'd been right. What he felt was gratitude, not love. Her only desire was that in the future he would think kindly of her.

Days took on a regular pattern. She rose early and continued with her running, sometimes going as far as three miles.

Her work offered few challenges. Patients were shuffled in and out of the treatment room every fifteen minutes, sometimes longer, depending on the nature of the damage. The clinic specialized in treating sports injuries. Usually little more than ice packs, electric muscle stimulation, and a work-out schedule with weights. But there was little personal satisfaction.

Usually Joy didn't eat until late in the evening. Her appetite was nearly nonexistent. Clara's good cooking had spoiled her, and when it came to fixing herself something to eat it was easier to open a can or toss something in the oven.

Friday night, after a long week, Joy left the front door of the apartment open while she sat drinking from a glass of iced tea, her leg draped over the side of her chair. Her attention flittered over the glossy pages of a woman's magazine.

When the doorbell buzzed, Joy assumed it was Danielle, who sometimes stopped in unexpectedly. Unlooping her leg, she set the tea aside and sauntered to the door.

The welcome died on her lips. Was she hallucinating? Dreaming? Sloan, standing erect without the aid of crutches or walker, stood before her.

Dressed in tan slacks and a blue knit shirt, he looked compelling and handsome. The vigorous masculine features broke into a ready smile.

"Hello, my Joy." The lazy, warm voice assured her that her mind wasn't playing cruel tricks.

"Sloan." His name slipped from her lips as the magazine fell to the floor. She stooped to retrieve it, conscious of her rolled-up cotton pants and bare feet.

"Aren't you going to invite me in?"

"Of course," she muttered, her voice trembling as her fingers fumbled with the lock on the screen door. "You're using the cane." The observation wasn't one of her most brilliant. But she knew how hard he must have worked in the three weeks since she'd last seen him to be using the cane.

"Yes, but only for a few days." The limp was barely noticeable as he walked into the room.

"You're doing great." It was so good to see him that she had to restrain herself from throwing her arms around him. Her heart was singing a rhapsody.

"Thanks."

Her hands were clenched self-consciously in front of her. "Would you like something to drink? I made some fresh iced tea earlier. From scratch, the way Clara does."

"That sounds fine."

Joy felt like skipping into the kitchen. Her mind whirled at the virile sight of him. He looked magnificent. Oh heavens, why hadn't she washed her hair tonight? She was a mess.

"Make yourself comfortable," she said, and motioned toward the chair she'd vacated. "I'll only be a minute."

Joy had opened the refrigerator door and taken out the pitcher of tea before she noticed that Sloan had followed her.

"Aren't you going to admit it's good to see me?" His gaze shimmered over her.

"It is," she said, and beamed him a bright smile. "It really is. You look great."

"So do you."

The tea made a swishing sound at the bottom of the glass as she poured it over the ice cubes. Her hand shook as she added a lemon slice to the side of the tall glass. When she held it out for him, Sloan's hand cupped hers.

"I've missed you, my Joy."

"And I've missed you." She forced a light gaiety into her voice.

Sloan set the tea on the formica counter without releasing her hand. His eyes held her prisoner as he tugged gently on her arm, bringing her closer to his side.

"I want you to come back."

"Oh, Sloan," she murmured miserably, and dropped her gaze. "You don't need me; I can't come back."

"I love you, Joy. I've loved you from the time you held up your head and walked out of the pool, letting me see your scars. Proud, regal, and so beautiful I nearly drowned just watching you."

"Don't, Sloan, please." She injected a plea into his name.

"I can't change the way I feel. I love you."

Backed against the kitchen counter, she was grateful for the support it gave her. "Listen to me, please."

"No," he said, and sighed heavily. "I listened to you the last time. Now it's my turn."

"All right." Her hesitation was pronounced. She didn't want this, but there was little choice. Nothing he could say would change her mind.

"I know what you're thinking."

"I'm sure you don't—"

"It isn't gratitude," he interrupted her, his voice heavy with building frustration. "We're a team; we have been almost from the day you arrived. We were even injured in the same kind of accident. I could have fallen off a cliff skiing or broken my back a hundred different ways. But I didn't. We like the same things, share the same ideals. I am thankful for what you did, I can't deny that, but it's so much more."

"I'm a therapist." She placed her palm across her breast in an identifying action. "I've worked in tons of cases like yours. Patients always fall in love with their therapists. It's common knowledge that it happens all the time."

"In other words, I'm one of the scores who have fallen for you."

"It isn't a true emotion, but one prompted by appreciation for what I've done."

Sloan took in a deep, angry breath. "In this case I think you outdid yourself," he returned flatly.

"Your parents' bonus check was very generous." Her heart was crying with the agony she was causing them both.

The handsome face was twisted with bitterness. "You're wrong. I know what I feel. I'm not a young boy suffering from my first case of puppy love." His voice was low and rough with frustration, almost angry.

"The thing is, we've been through a lot together. We've worked hard; I've seen you at your best and your worst. You've shared a part of yourself with me that probably few others

have ever seen. It's only natural that you
would come to think you love me. Believe me
when I say sincerely that I've never been more
honored.''

"Don't say that. I want to share my life with
yours. I want you to be the mother of my children and stand by my side in the years ahead.
When I wake up at night, I want to feel your
softness at my side. Tell me you don't want this
too.''

"Sloan." Tears blurred her eyes as she lifted
her gaze. She loved him desperately and at the
same time hated him for what he was forcing
her to do. Perhaps now he wanted these things.
But later that would change. His gratefulness
would diminish and he'd realize what a terrible mistake he'd made.

"Say it, Joy. Tell me you want me." His
hands, warm and possessive, cupped her
shoulders.

"You're being unfair." Her throat felt raw,
and it throbbed.

"I'm being more than fair. All I ask is a
simple straightforward answer. I love you; I
want to marry you. Yes or no?''

She stood, unable to formulate the word,
not when every part of her was crying out for

her to go to him. A huge lump had a strangle-hold on her voice.

"Joy?" he prompted. "Just say yes." His voice was a caressing whisper. His fingers pressed lightly into her shoulder as if that would encourage her.

Tightly she closed her eyes, unable to bear looking at him. A tear squeezed through her lashes and ran down her cheek.

With infinite tenderness, Sloan kissed the moisture away.

"No." Somehow the word managed to slip out. Joy felt his shock.

"I see." He dropped his hands from her shoulders. She blinked through a curtain of tears. "I'm sorry; so sorry." She felt raw and vulnerable.

"Not to worry." The grim voice was cutting. "I appreciate the honesty." He turned abruptly and moved out of the kitchen.

Dazed, hurt, dying, Joy watched him leave as the tears slid down her face. He didn't hesitate.

Ten

Mutely Joy walked to the screen door to catch one last glimpse of Sloan as he strolled out of her life. His limp was more pronounced now, his shoulders hunched. Joy bit viciously into her bottom lip, and the taste of blood filled her mouth. Never had anything been more difficult; never had anything been more right.

Someday the hurt would go away and she would be stronger for it. At least that was what Joy told herself repeatedly in the long, dark days that followed. She had no energy. Listlessly she laid around the house. Food held no appeal, and she began skipping meals. Her weight began to drop. She wouldn't allow herself the luxury of tears. The decision had been made; she had done the right thing. It would be useless to cry over it now.

Five days after Sloan's visit there was no doubt that summer had arrived in southern California. Heat and humidity filled the tiny apartment, and Joy turned on a fan in hopes the small appliance would stir the heavy heat.

The thin cotton blouse stuck to her skin, and she unfastened the second button. Perspiration rolled down the hollow between her breasts.

Impatiently she walked into the kitchen and took a soft drink out of the refrigerator. Empty calories for an empty life, she mused as she ripped the pull tab from the aluminum can.

The phone rang, and she felt like plugging her ears. There wasn't anyone she wanted to talk to. Not her mother. Not her brother. Not even Danielle. No one. The whole attitude was so unlike her that Joy knew it was important to shed this dark apathy as quickly as possible.

"Hello." Her voice held little welcome.

"Hi, Joy. This is Paul. How you doing?"

"Paul," she spoke into the mouthpiece, surprise raising her tone. "I'm fine. How are you?"

"Great. Listen, I know this is sudden and all, but how about dinner? We could meet at Mobey Jake's."

"I...I don't know." She hesitated. Why torture herself? Paul was sure to mention Sloan.

"Have you eaten?"

"No. It's too hot to eat."

"Come on," Paul encouraged. "It's the least you can do, since I didn't get so much as a good-bye when you left. That still rankles." He was playful and teasing.

Joy laughed, and the sound surprised her. It'd been weeks since she'd found anything amusing. "All right," she agreed, "but give me an hour."

"Do you want me to pick you up, or can you meet me?"

"I'll meet you."

Mobey Jake's held fond memories. The flashing neon whale, round tables with faded umbrellas, and some of the best fried fish on the California coast. The first barrier she had hurdled in her relationship with Sloan had been the night she had brought him an order of fish from Mobey Jake's. Even L.J. had liked this fish the best. And who could blame him?

Joy was sitting at a table that overlooked the seashore far below when Paul arrived. He came from the direction of the beach home, which answered Joy's first uncertainty. Paul was still with Sloan. Had Sloan sent him to talk to her? As soon as the question formed, she knew the answer. Sloan did his own talking.

Paul parked the older-model convertible and waved. Joy returned the gesture. He looked fit, tan, and muscular.

Tucking the car keys in his jean pocket, he smiled as he strolled toward her. "You look good." The hesitation was slight enough for her to notice.

"I don't, either."

"Lost weight?"

"A few pounds." Her fingers curled around the tall Styrofoam cup. "I'm ready to order." She changed the subject abruptly, not wanting to be the topic of their conversation.

She waited while Paul stood in line at the window and placed the order for their meal. He returned a few minutes later with their standard. Joy looked at the large double order of fish, knowing there wasn't an L.J. to eat the leftovers. The memory of her little friend tightened her stomach.

"I don't suppose you've seen L.J.?" She looked up at Paul.

"That darn bird of yours? No, I haven't."

"I wonder what ever became of him."

Paul shrugged his shoulders and slipped a large piece of fish into his mouth. Avoiding her gaze, he looked out over the scenery. "Don't you wonder about anyone else?"

Deliberately obtuse, Joy returned, "Of course, I do. How's Clara?"

"Ready to quit."

"Clara? I don't believe it. She's been with the Whittakers for years."

"Neither one of us can take much more of what's been going on lately."

Joy nearly choked on a french fry. "Oh?"

"Aren't you interested?"

"I don't know," Joy managed to sound offhand and unconcerned, when she was terrified Paul would even mention Sloan's name.

"I understand where you're coming from," he began, "and whatever's between you and Sloan is none of my business, but something's got to be done."

"What do you mean?"

Paul took a swig of beer and with deliberate casualness placed it back on the table. "I shouldn't trouble you with this. After all, you were the smart one to get out when you did."

"Paul!" For the first time, Joy wanted to shake the younger man. "Obviously there's something you want me to know. Now either get it over with or shut up."

"It's Whittaker." Paul sounded uncertain now.

"Well for heaven's sake, who else would be causing you any problems?" Joy was quickly losing her patience.

Paul avoided her gaze, fingering the fish. "He's in a bad way."

"How do you mean? Did he fall and hurt himself? Why didn't anyone let me know? Paul, does he need me?" All her concerns rushed out in one giant breath.

"He needs you all right, but not because of any fall."

"What do you mean?"

"I wish I knew. Listen, I don't know what happened last week, but Whittaker hasn't been the same since he came back from seeing you."

Joy hadn't been the same either. "How's that?"

"For nearly three weeks he practically killed himself—and me," Paul added sheepishly, "so that he could walk with the cane. His goal was to come to you. He never said as much, mind you, but it was understood. I don't know what you said, or what *he* said, for that matter, but Sloan's been locked up in his room ever since.''

"I don't believe it.''

"It's true. Ask Clara. He shouts and throws things at anyone who comes near him. If you think he was an angry beast when you first came, you should see him now. I think he's drinking pretty heavy, too.''

"Oh, no.'' Joy's shoulders sagged. "Oh, Paul, no.''

Joy hardly slept that night. Everything Paul told her seemed to press against her as she tossed and turned fitfully.

Before the sun came up the next morning, she was dressed in her uniform, the one she wore while working with Sloan. The ride down the highway was accomplished in short order, and she pulled into the long driveway that led to the beach house. Pausing, she looked apprehensively at the closed drapes and prayed that she was doing the right thing.

Clara answered her timid knock and gave a cry of welcome when she saw it was Joy.

"I'm so glad you've come.'' She hugged Joy briefly and hurried on to explain. "I just didn't know what to do for Mr. Whittaker any more.

He doesn't want to see no one. He hardly eats and keeps himself locked up in that room. Not even his father, not no one. But he'll see you, Joy. It's you Mr. Whittaker needs.''

Joy's returning hug lacked confidence. "If he thinks I went through months of work so he can lock himself away and sulk, then I'll tell him differently.''

"That-t-a girl.'' Clara patted her across her back. "I'll be in the kitchen cooking breakfast. Mr. Whittaker will eat now that you're here.''

"You do that.''

"I'll fix my best blueberry waffles. I'll cook some up for you too.''

Food was the last thing that occupied her thoughts, but Joy gave the old woman an encouraging nod.

Hands knotted at her side, Joy squared her shoulders and marched down the hall to Sloan's room. Boldly she knocked long and hard against his door.

"I said leave me alone.''

Pushing in the door, Joy was immediately assaulted with the stale and unpleasant odor of tobacco and beer. Wrinkling her nose, she proceeded into the room. Dirty clothes littered the floor, the bed was unmade, and the sheets hung off the edges.

In the dim interior, Joy didn't see Sloan at first. When he spoke, her attention was drawn across the room to the far corner. He sat in the wheelchair, the cane laying on the floor at his side. Two or more days' growth of beard darkened his face. His normally neatly styled hair was tangled and unruly. Paul hadn't been exaggerating when he said Sloan was in a bad way.

"What do you want?" The anger was unable to disguise his shock.

Joy didn't answer him; instead she walked across the room and pulled open the drapes. Brilliant sunlight chased away the shadows and filled the room with its golden rays.

"Get out of here, Joy."

"No." Hands on hips, she whirled around. "What's the matter with you?"

He didn't bother to answer. Instead he stood, limped across the room, and closed the drapes. "Wasn't it you who said if I wanted to keep the drapes closed I'd have to do it myself? I just have. Now get out."

"Oh no you don't," she flared, and jerked the drapes open a second time. Not an inch separated them.

Sloan squinted with the light. "Who the hell let you in here anyway? They'll pay with their job when I find out."

"What's that doing sitting in here?" She pointed to the wheelchair. "When I left, it was because you would never need that thing again." Now she was angry, just as angry as Sloan.

"Is that what it takes to bring you back in my life? A wheelchair?"

"No," she cried. "But I didn't spend long, hard weeks working with you so that you could sit in the dark."

"I thought I told you to get out of here. This is my life, and I'll live it as I please," he shouted back harshly.

"Not when I've invested my time in it you won't."

"Damn, where is that bottle? I need a drink." A hand against the side of his head, he looked around the room, carelessly throwing clothes and anything that impeded the search.

"Alcohol is the last thing you need."

"Go home, little girl. I don't want you."

"Sloan, for heaven's sake, look at what you're doing to yourself. This is ridiculous."

"No more crazy than your coming here. I don't need your devotion or your pity."

"Pity?" she nearly choked on the word. "I can't believe you'd even suggest anything like that."

"You've made your feelings crystal clear," he told her roughly. "If it isn't sympathy, what is it?"

Joy pressed her lips together.

"Why?" he demanded a second time.

"I...I don't know why," she lied, and stalked across the room, arms hugging her waist. He shouted at her again, and she grimaced, not even hearing the words. "All right," she cried, "you want to know why? I'll tell you. I didn't go through the agony of giving you back to the Trixies of the world so you could waste your life."

"Have you gone crazy?"

"Yes, I'm nuts, and another week like last one and I'll be carted off to the loony bin." She knew she was being irrational, but she had lost the power to reason. She didn't know what she'd planned to say when she walked into his room. But nothing was going right, and everything looked so hopeless.

"Joy." An incredulous note entered his voice. "Do you love me?"

Joy opened her mouth to deny herself again, but the words wouldn't come.

"Do you?"

"Yes," she snapped.

"You idiot. You crazy idiot," he muttered, and pulled her into his arms, his hold strong and sure. He expelled a rush of air and relaxed against her.

Somehow Joy had never heard anything more beautiful.

"Why did you send me away?" His breath stirred the hair at the crown of her head.

She slid her arms around his neck, reveling in the feel of his body close to hers. "I couldn't let you waste yourself on a nobody like me because you're grateful."

His arms tightened around her. "Grateful." He spat the word out. "I've come to almost hate that word. What does it take to convince you that what I feel is love?"

"Thirty years?" she breathed, and laid her head against the muscular chest.

"'That's not near long enough," he told her huskily, his hand weaving in the short curls, pressing her to him.

"But, Sloan, how can you love me? I'm not pretty or rich or—"

"Stop," he interrupted her, almost angry again. "I love you, and I won't have you saying those things about yourself. When you first came, for all intents and purposes I was crippled. Then I was walking again, and you left. Everything should have been perfect, but I was more of a cripple without you."

"But I don't fit in—"

"The only thing that's going to stop you from arguing with me is kissing you."

She laughed and nuzzled his neck. "That might work," she said shakily, and raised her head to meet his descending mouth. Her lips parted under his, and the blood rushed through her veins. No longer did she question if Sloan's feelings were interwoven with a deep sense of appreciation. He loved her; she knew that now as intuitively as she had recognized her own feelings.

Possessively his hands slid over the womanly curves of her ribcage to cup the swelling fullness of her breasts. He shuddered and buried his face in her neck. "You'll marry me." It wasn't a question, but a statement of fact.

"Yes," she breathed in happily. "Oh, yes."

"Children?"

"As many as you want."

"My, my, you're agreeable."

"All right, no more than ten."

He rubbed his chin along the top of her head. "You won't go away if I take a shower and change clothes, will you?"

Her arms curved around the broad expanse of his chest. "Are you kidding? You've given me enough reason to hang around for a lifetime."

Chuckling, he kissed the top of her nose. "Are you always going to be this stubborn?"

"You'll find out," she teased.

"I can hardly wait."

An hour later, their arms looped around each other's waist, they slowly sauntered down the flawless beach. Their bare feet made deep indentations in the sand, their footsteps punctuated by Sloan's cane.

A brisk breeze whipped a curl across Joy's face. Sloan tucked it around her ear and kissed her hard and deep.

"I love you," she told him shakily, her voice still affected by his kiss.

"I wondered how long it would take you to say it."

"I admitted it to myself a long time ago."

Above, a flock of sea gulls circled and let out a loud squawk. Joy paused and shielded her eyes with her hand.

"Sloan," she whispered in disbelief. "It's L.J."

"Honey, there are a thousand birds out here that look exactly like him."

"He's up there. That's him," she cried, pointing him out for Sloan. Happiness trapped the oxygen in her lungs. "It's got to be him."

"Joy." Sloan arched both brows.

Her attention was directed to the flock of birds that flew down the beach. Only one stayed behind, landing a few feet away.

"It is him," she whispered.

"You didn't tell me I would be forced to fight off flocks of admirers," Sloan teased with a smile of intense satisfaction.

L.J. quirked his head as if to say he didn't have time to chat, spread his wings, and flew back to his friends.

"He just stopped by to say hello," Joy murmured happily.

"And I," Sloan whispered, pulling her into his arms, "have come to stay a lifetime."